A Compromised Compromise

Timothy Underwood

ACKNOWLEDGMENTS

As always I want to thank my dear beta readers, who caught several important problems in this book. Betty Jo and mandieschwaderer looked at the book and DJ Hendrickson did the copy edit. I also want to thank my fiance, Sára Vitrai for supporting me and always telling me that she is proud of me, and for not complaining when I experiment with different writing schedules, or finish up a scene when the writing is going well in bed with a dim screen after one in the morning.

Prologue

During the first month after she became engaged to Mr. Darcy, Elizabeth placed harsh and sometimes resentful blame upon the rug in the Netherfield library.

This thick lush rug was made from the fur of a bear with the claws still attached. The unfortunate animal had been a victim of the newly minted baronet who built Netherfield. This dapper nabob, flush with the stolen wealth of the Indies (both East and West), killed the impressive animal during a hunt on the continent where such wild beasts yet roamed free. His wife smilingly nodded at her husband's manly exploits when he returned to merry green England with the rug, but disliking all forms of taxidermy, she stoutly refused to have it placed in *her* drawing room, or her dining room, or anywhere else she liked to spend time.

This happenstance occurred many years before, but this baronet and his family were no more enthused by books than Mr. Bingley, to whom the baronet's great nephew had recently let the stuffy old pile so he could afford to spend all his time with lushly disreputable opera singers in an almost fashionable district of London.

In the decades since the brave continental quest to shoot the first owner of the skin and soft fur that made the rug had come to its successful conclusion, the rug had been removed and beaten for dust and thoroughly washed as needed, but had never been replaced nor used to any great point. Sadly for the baronet, after an incident that left one of the baronet's daughters with a small permanent scar on her arm, the teeth had been removed from the bear's head, and the claws declawed.

Elizabeth thought the rug delightfully grotesque when her eyes lit upon it while she spent an uncomfortable hour in the library with Mr. Darcy, during which he did not once lift his eyes from his book, even though Elizabeth, much as she was determined in her heart to loathe the man, was constantly aware of his presence. Her eyes going everywhere but Mr. Darcy absently fell upon the head of the bear, and she wondered if anyone had ever tripped over it. Such a thing did not belong in the middle of a library, but in a male den choked with cigar smoke and the smell of spilt port where women were never permitted.

Promptly Elizabeth forgot about the matter and the tripping danger, and returned to her pretence of reading as she paid attention to how Mr. Darcy paid no attention to her.

Mr. Darcy on the other hand never thought at all about the rug which would govern his fate, as his mind was brimming to the top with thoughts of the unsuitability of Miss Elizabeth Bennet the unsuitable.

Upon such objects can the fate of men turn.

Later Elizabeth changed her mind, and during their honeymoon she convinced Mr. Darcy that everything which happened was an inevitable consequence of their true emotions and fate, and they would have *somehow* determined to marry each other, even if the presence of the rug had made this event sooner, and perhaps more tumultuous, than it otherwise would have been.

Chapter One

On the night of the Netherfield Ball, late in the evening, after the supper party had seen Mrs. Bennet thoroughly embarrass herself, Mr. Darcy took into his head that he needed to explain everything, or at least enough, about Mr. Wickham's proclivities to warn Elizabeth, in case she was on the course to fall into an infatuation with Wickham. Darcy's emotion towards Elizabeth was such that he did not believe the scoundrel could seduce her, but he did not wish to see her heart broken, and the more he thought about Wickham, the more he wished to explain and defend himself to *Elizabeth*, even though it was below him to do so.

For the purpose of having privacy to allow Mr. Darcy to defend with private particulars his interactions with Wickham, the two of them sought private council in the library, with just a few candles flickering on the indiawood table for light. In this dim light it became almost impossible to see the grinning, toothless maw of the bear.

"Now *explain*. How can you possibly justify your horrid treatment of Mr. Wickham?"

Fitzwilliam Darcy stared with apparent coldness, but in fact from a deep well of passion, at Elizabeth Bennet, as the candle light flickered tantalizingly and seductively on her delicate face. The violins of the ball whispered sweet melodies through the closed door.

He should not tell the details about Georgiana, even though he trusted Elizabeth.

She had been strangely angry at him during their dance — Darcy was reasonably certain she became angry mainly because she realized he would not allow his passionate interest in her to override his capable judgement and good reason and cause him to make an offer to her. But if his real intention was to have nothing further to do with her, *why* in the name of his good name whose tarnish he risked with this conference was he closeted alone with her during a ball?

However, Darcy reassured himself, he was not jealous of Mr. Wickham. Obviously Elizabeth could not care anything for Mr. Wickham, and that her violent defence of the slithering scoundrel sprung from her unquenchable desire for Darcy (and his wealth), and her knowledge that she would never gain her end.

She suffered, no doubt, from the same panging pain that pierced his own chest, but the weaker spirit of a woman could not handle such feelings with equanimity and a calm cold countenance.

Darcy realized as Elizabeth stared at him, her look changing from anger to something else, that he had not spoken in reply.

The candlelights seductively flickered in the deep mysterious mirrors of her eyes.

"He seduces women." Darcy's voice was low, involuntarily seductive. Darcy tried to roughen his voice. He needed to avoid any such hint of feeling or desire towards the unsuitable, yet perfectly desirable maiden. "For marriage he wishes a *fortune*. He can have no serious interest in you."

Darcy grimaced internally, as Elizabeth's eyes flashed angrily.

He knew enough of the vanity of women to know that telling them that any man was not the thrall of their love was certain to raise their ire. He had once attempted to explain the lack of interest on the part of a third party to Caroline Bingley, when she had been sufficiently repelled by his unresponsiveness to her flirtations to dangle her bonnet towards the heir of an earldom.

Miss Bingley had been quite displeased with him when he suggested that the Viscount had no interest in her. Unfortunately she then determined that Darcy's caution to her was a sign of his jealousy, and thus his interest in her, and he'd not been able to get her to stop simpering after his approval since.

No! He did not want to give Elizabeth false hopes. He should have found a different route to condemn Wickham than one which would inevitably lead Elizabeth to believe that *he,* Darcy, had designs upon her.

"Proof." Elizabeth clenched her jaw, the muscles spasming with anger. "Proof. When you make such accusations against a man enormously below you, proof is expected."

"I have seen him at university, and when we were at Eton and in the village around Pemberley when we were young men. He is obsessed with women, and he has had surprising success…" Darcy trailed off. As a boy he *had* been jealous of Wickham's ease with women. "From the instant he awoke to an awareness that a man could desire a woman," Darcy continued in a firm voice, "his sole pursuit has been the seduction of female virtues, and the destruction of female honor. And money. And opportunities to gamble. He also drinks a great deal. And he wasted his opportunity to study law."

"*Proof.* Something beyond your word."

"I am not in the habit of having my honorable word questioned. You have seen me and spoken with me, and my character is without question. What good have you seen of Wickham?"

"His manner!" Elizabeth then became still and quiet and spoke in a sharp voice that almost scared Darcy. "I have spoken with him, and judged him as friendly, and kind, and open. You have nothing but arrogance, and ungentlemanliness, and harsh words. And you wonder why I trust him more?"

"You *trust* Wickham?" Darcy sneered and snorted. Obviously she just said *that* to place a thorn in his socks to dig at the delicate skin.

"Why should I not? Your *father* trusted him."

Darcy winced, remembering how he'd asked the servants to tell nothing to Papa as he lay dying about Wickham's seduction of a servant girl in a neighboring estate. It would have done his father no good to know, and Darcy wanted to spare his father the knowledge of his favorite's indiscretion and callousness — Wickham refused to even *speak* with the girl after she named him. Perhaps he should have then taken the actions that would have led to Wickham being removed from the will and his life earlier.

Besides, in honor, Papa had promised Wickham enough that they owed Wickham some chance at education. Darcy was glad Wickham had wasted his chance.

"Ha!" Elizabeth cried. "You know your father was a better man than you."

"My father was a better man than us all. But my sadness is at the knowledge of how disappointed he would be in Wickham if he knew. I hid from him, in his final months, my knowledge of Wickham's true behavior. Of the women he had seduced, and of the—"

"What *proof* do you have?"

Darcy sneered. "You are entirely decided against me. It is not my place to bow and scrape and prove to you the truth, when you do not wish to listen. You have been warned. You may set my character against his, and decide what to trust."

"Enough." Elizabeth angrily hissed, "I shall leave now, and have nothing further to do with you."

Her eyes told a different tale.

She didn't want to leave. They glared at each other, panting heavily.

Her eyes slowly widened. Somehow their faces were drifting towards each other.

Elizabeth bit her lip and stiffened her back and turning round, she angrily, yet blushingly, walked forward towards the door.

No. He couldn't let her leave, not while she was this angry at him. And not when she might still be Wickham's besotted thrall.

Elizabeth angrily trod away, stepping, without paying attention to it, past the ridiculous bear rug on the floor.

Whoooooops.

Darcy saw, like in slow motion, her pretty silver satin slipper catch on the bear's jaw. She fell forward, flailing her arms out and holding her hands in front to catch her.

Without thought Darcy shot forward. He grabbed her with his wide hands around the waist and caught her in his arms before she thudded on the ground.

Her body. In his arms.

Her sweet, warm, fragrant, panting body.

In his arms.

His fingers inches away from her breasts, the bare skin of her open back against his ungloved palm.

Their faces inches apart as he pulled her to stand without letting go of her.

Their eyes stared into each other.

They moved at the same moment, their lips pressed against each other, in a powerful kiss neither controlled. With desperate passion he pulled her tight against him, he gripped her bum and pressed her hips against his, he felt her soft length against his harder body. They kissed and kissed. A distant part of his mind knew that this was wrong, and that he did not wish to fulfill the promise to her that his body wished to make.

She whimpered as his tongue slid briefly along her sweet upper lip.

Darcy's brain was too full of her taste to do what he must — thrust her away, and tell her to never speak to him again, as he could not control himself in her presence.

They continued to kiss, wetly and hungrily, with more passion than he had ever felt before. His tongue licked along her lips and touched her tongue.

The door to library quietly opened, and there were long seconds of continued passionate kissing before Darcy registered that they were no longer alone.

And before he and Elizabeth could fully leap apart, Mrs. Bennet's shrill voice cried out, "Lizzy and Mr. Darcy kissing! Oh!"

Both Darcy and Elizabeth stared at her.

Mr. Bingley and Sir William stood next to Mrs. Bennet. Mr. Bingley's eyes were wide and he started to slyly grin. Darcy still gripped Elizabeth in his arms, her hand was still around his neck, and they both were still too startled to move.

Mrs. Bennet happily added, "Heavens! As good as a Lord! So much better than Mr. Collins! I would have made you marry *him*, Lizzy, but clever girl, you knew you had better prospects."

*****

Elizabeth felt numb, dizzy, and as if everything was surreal in the minutes after they interrupted the surprising kiss. A kiss during which she learned several important matters: First, she did not hate Mr. Darcy; Second, she *was* handsome enough to tempt him; and finally, she *really* did not hate Mr. Darcy.

Everything happened so fast, giving Elizabeth no time to contemplate those concerning revelations.

They were surrounded suddenly by well-wishers as her mother cried out again, again, and again that they were marrying. She looked at Darcy, terrified both that he would leave her suddenly jilted and with her reputation in tatters after three people saw them kissing passionately, and almost as scared that he would agree and make no objection.

Darcy's face was his hard mask, and Elizabeth suddenly realized that was his way of allowing him to think. He felt something — he felt as confused and conflicted as she did.

That was visible to her in his eyes somehow.

But he did not want everyone to see his confusion. He always, she realized in that moment of clarity, he always needed to appear in command, the grand, arrogant master of Pemberley, even if he was a young man, a young person, like everyone else. He looked like an arrogant aristocrat silently disdaining the congratulations of her neighbors, when that was *not* what he felt at all.

But what was he thinking?

He did not deny that they were to marry.

Mr. Bennet came up, and he angrily looked at them. "What is this about?" He first looked at Elizabeth for an answer.

The room was too stuffy. Too many candles had burned too long, and all the fresh air was gone. The windows were all closed up against the late November cold. The band played a quick Irish air whose upbeat mood clashed with Elizabeth's torn feelings. She was numb, like someone who'd received a wound in a carriage accident, but was still too occupied stumbling around surprised at their survival to notice that they may not have survived.

"Mr. Darcy and Lizzy are to marry! Isn't that wonderful, Mr. Bennet! He's as good as a Lord!"

"Nonsense," Mr. Bennet replied in a rolling voice. "Lizzy doesn't like him at all. Mr. Darcy does not look at anyone except to disdain."

"I understand your surprise, sir." Darcy stood taller. The first words he had said since he caught her in his arms and kissed her. "Matters have been so arranged that I have no choice."

"*What* occurred?

Elizabeth blushed and looked at her neighbors surrounding them. She couldn't exclaim in front of them all that it was an accident. A mistake. They didn't mean to kiss. At least Darcy would marry her, thus saving her the terrible embarrassment today of them knowing she'd kissed him like that without any agreement, or even words that were not angry.

"Miss Elizabeth and Mr. Darcy," Sir William spoke smilingly, "were caught in a quite pretty embrace when we went to enter the library. Your wife had wanted to talk with me and Mr. Bingley about plans for the next assembly ball, and—"

"Ha. I thought so." Darcy spoke firmly, as if something he had been certain of before was now proven to everyone's satisfaction. He stood tall in his fine green wool coat, with his surprisingly soft, yet well-muscled hands tightly gripped together behind his back.

"Thought *what*?" Mr. Bennet asked for Elizabeth.

Darcy looked towards Elizabeth and tilted his head with a sarcastic smile that somehow let her know exactly what he was thinking: he had decided that she had planned to be interrupted while kissing him by her mother, so that he would have no choice but to marry him.

Elizabeth ground her teeth so that her cheeks ached. "Ridiculous — I can tell what you are thinking — what you assume is completely wrong."

Darcy looked down at her from where he perched his head so high up on top of his shoulders. This time he *was* being intentionally disdainful. There was a chatter as people chatted excitedly, the echoes bouncing off the wooden walls, but the bustling crowd allowed her, Papa, and Mr. Darcy to speak together in something vaguely like privacy.

Elizabeth felt faint. She could not believe this had happened.

"How did it happen that you two — two persons who so far as I knew had never spoken a friendly word to each other — came to *embrace* each other in a room alone during a ball."

Darcy deigned not reply.

Mr. Bennet glared at his daughter. "Well, Lizzy? I expect better sense from *you*."

Elizabeth's blush travelled from her cheeks down her neck to meet another embarrassed flush at the top of her chest. "It well, just... well it just happened."

"*What* just happened? There is more to this tale than you are telling so far."

"Mr. Bennet," Darcy spoke calmly, glancing around at their neighbors. "If you wish me to impart all the details of what your *daughter* and your *wife* have done to create this situation, since you make a pretence — perhaps a true pretence — of ignorance, I will disclose all to you, but in a private situation. Not here."

Mr. Bennet's face clouded angrily, but he curtly nodded back. "Tomorrow morning. In my study. I shall expect to see you promptly."

Chapter Two

The next morning, Mr. Bingley laughed at Darcy when they both woke early (that is before eleven, the ball had continued quite late, almost into the dawn, the previous night), and he clapped Darcy on his back. "Damned fine girl, Miss Lizzy. Damned fine girl. Ha! You gave her a damned fine kiss."

Bingley grinned merrily at Darcy's sleep deprived glare. "No, no, no! This time *you* are on the back foot, and I'll not let you forget it soon. But off to London on my business. I'll be back in just a few. Give your lady love, and her *sisters*, especially her *one* sister my greetings, and express eagerness to see them all again."

What could Darcy say?

He had determined during the night that he absolutely had no choice but to marry Elizabeth, and thus for appearances he must only show the part of himself which was entirely happy to do so. Darcy grinned thinly, "I was caught on the back foot last night. Quite, quite caught. I shall deliver your greetings to Elizabeth."

It was a contemplative half hour ride to Longbourn.

Darcy smiled sardonically to himself. Mr. Bennet had been quite surprised by the behavior of his daughter.

Upon arriving, before he had chance to even knock upon the door, Mr. Collins waddled out of the house. Clearly the overweight vicar had been waiting for him. "Mr. Darcy! Mr. Darcy! Esteemed nephew of my beneficent patroness."

Well, he could at least forgive her in part for that. She would have needed to marry Mr. Collins if she had not so neatly trapped him. And Mr. Collins was an *ample* inducement to matrimony with *anyone* else. Darcy giggled internally at his low pun — Mr. Collins was *large, and ample* — but he only showed his amusement through a dry quirk of his lips that would over the years become unspeakably dear and familiar to Elizabeth.

But none of them knew that happy future yet.

"I have heard such rumors, such ridiculous rumors, as cannot be true. For as you know very well, you are to marry Miss Anne de Bourgh, the—"

"I am not going to marry Cousin Anne."

"Of course you are. The marriage was planned, as her Ladyship herself has discoursed many times, whilst in your cradles—"

Darcy had an image flash into his mind of Lady Catherine and his mother standing next to each other in the large and stable cradles they had built for their children, while Lady Catherine imperiously declared that he was to marry Anne, and his mother nodded along as the grand lady spoke. "Yes, that would be a very nice thing if it were to happen, but they really must *like* each other."

"I have neither," Darcy said calmly, "obligation of heart, nor honor, nor family feeling, to tie myself to my Cousin Anne. I further have neither desire nor wish to do so. I will become extremely dissatisfied with you, and I shall communicate this dissatisfaction to my aunt—" The aunt Darcy was thinking of was Lady Matlock. After Lady Catherine learned about his marriage, for at least a six-month anything he might say to the detriment of her clergyman would be taken in the opposite spirit, that of a recommendation, by her. "—if I hear you to say anything about this supposed engagement to anyone at all."

"But... but I have already told the entire family that it is impossible you should marry Miss Elizabeth, who is nearly betrothed to me."

Darcy almost vomited at imagining Elizabeth kissing this toad the way she had kissed him. She kissed him deceitfully, yes, but also passionately, the previous night.

"So you see," Mr. Collins whined, "you must explain this mistake to them all."

"Mr. Collins!" Darcy's voice slapped him like a thunderclap, before dropping into a low menacing quiet. "You interfere in matters above your station. Do not let my aunt's condescension make you think you have place to comment upon *my* honor and *my* behaviors. Or to aspire in the slightest way to the hand or interest of *my* betrothed. I am to marry Miss Elizabeth, and I shall hear nothing further upon these matters from you."

"Oh, my. Oh my." Mr. Collins pulled compulsively at his clerical collar, as though it was choking him. "Oh, she will not be happy. Not at all. And I am here. She will not be happy. She would expect me to stop it — Mr. Darcy, I was told by Mrs. Bennet that she looked favorably upon my marriage with—"

"Silence." Darcy's voice cracked like a gunshot.

Mr. Darcy walked raging past Mr. Collins. It made him to think more kindly, again, upon Elizabeth. It was disturbingly easy to forgive the game she had played against him, and the trap she had placed him in. Especially on this consideration that she would have been forced to marry Mr. Collins by her mother if a more suitable suitor had not presented his suit.

He ought not forgive her so easy.

She did not deserve his forgiveness, and he must remind himself, no matter how sparkling her eyes, or passionate her lips, or sweet the feel of her slenderness and skin beneath his fingers. She was a low scheming woman, with a mind and honor quite below what he had thought.

Of course, he too was far beneath what he had thought himself to be. His self-control and sense of honor and propriety had been tested, and in the testing they had been found wanting.

No one deserved blame for this unwanted marriage except himself.

In his attraction to Elizabeth he had put himself in the position where she and her scheming mother could entrap him, and while she had pretended to "trip" into him, he had chosen to kiss her. Elizabeth had read the mind of her prey, and seen that he could be captured by this she-wolf of Longbourn.

As Darcy entered Mr. Bennet's smoky, musty, and yet bright study, Darcy's determination to think kindly upon the Bennets, as there was no choice, and as he had no one to blame but himself fell away at Mr. Bennet's first angry words.

"Mr. Darcy, you are not so respectable as I thought you." The balding man lightly slammed his palm on the surface of his worn and ink stained desk. "Not so respectable."

Darcy's jaw clenched. To be lectured by *this* man, this man who had raised such a scheming, fortune huntress of a daughter. Darcy confessed to himself that he deserved the insult, but a man such as Mr. Bennet should be silent. Bingley might speak so to him, or his cousin — he would even rather such an insult from *Wickham* than this man, whose family was to benefit enormously from the low scheming.

"You were found openly kissing *my daughter* in the library of Netherfield — not only my wife, but Sir William and your friend Mr. Bingley saw you — if it was just my wife, we would pretend the whole matter never happened, and I could happily toss you by your ears away."

"Ha! You desire to do no such thing."

"Have you anything to say for yourself? Anything to make me view the man who kissed my daughter, openly in a nearly public place, without any courtship, and without having spoken at all to me with less distaste as a son-in-law?"

"I am the victim in this matter." Mr. Darcy sneered. "If you insult me so, you shall find you cannot control me. I shall leave if I am pushed. It was your daughter's scheming, in combination with that of her mother, which brought me to this place. I have been entrapped neatly by them, but for you to further impugn my honor—"

"Trapped!" Mr. Bennet expostulated, and pounded his desk for emphasis. "You kissed my daughter."

"She kissed me."

"I very much doubt that. Her honor I know."

"She maneuvered so that she fell into my arms, and then she kissed me in return. Knowing that her mother, at that moment was waiting to enter the room and catch us together. Neatly done, and I have been trapped by my passion — I could not control such passion, though I ought have. That is my demerit. But I have acted, acted since I was entrapped by her and by my basest feelings, in the manner of a gentleman of honor. I am here, offering myself up to you as a husband for your—" Darcy squared his jaw "—your *clever* daughter. So take me, refuse me, but do *not* lecture me upon my how respectable I am. For your family is entirely disrespectable, while I act as a man, who is a man, ought to act."

Silence attacked the room when Darcy finished this speech.

Darcy neatly balanced on both feet with a wide stance, as he had not sat before Mr. Bennet insulted him. The room was warm, and embers glowed behind the grating of the stove.

Mr. Bennet seemed to have gained years in the past minute. His face appeared haggard and tired, with thin grey hairs falling neatly around his ears. He pulled off his spectacles and nervously wiped the lenses with a white cloth produced from a desk drawer.

Mr. Darcy waited, comfortable in Mr. Bennet's apparent discomfort.

At last Mr. Bennet resettled his spectacles upon his long nose, and pulled at one of his sideburns. "So that is it — eh. That is what you truly think of Lizzy?"

The old, wan and *scared* voice of the man struck Darcy like he had been tossed in a freezing pond, making him numb and shocked. Did he *really* think this about his Elizabeth? Who had kissed him so sweetly? And then remembering how she had manipulated him through that kiss, his proper rage returned.

"In what other manner ought I to think upon her?" Darcy spoke harshly. It was not his place to comfort the father of such a daughter, though once they were married, he would show her every courtesy and kindness, whilst never, never forgetting that she could not be trusted. "The facts are what the facts are."

"Had I any choice, any choice at all, I would refuse you permission. You two should not marry. Unhappily we are all trapped. After such a scene, everyone would assume the worst about both you and Elizabeth should such a marriage not occur, and for me it would destroy both her possibilities and those of her sisters. So I give you permission — but I beg you. Mr. Darcy, I beg you — think kinder of her. If my dear Lizzy is to be your wife, I beg you, learn to think kindly of her, and learn to see the truth."

"What truth? That my children will be clever in seeking their own ends, and that though they destroy the ancient honor and name of the Darcy family, they will no doubt seduce their way into marriages with Dukes and earls and gain great successes and other forms of base material gain? That they will have that weakness towards passion I have, but also the scheming cleverness of your—"

"That is not the truth of Lizzy. You should know that."

"She seduced me into kissing her. She seduced me such, so that your wife might find us. This is the plain nature of the matter. I am a rational man; I can think nothing else. I shall marry her, sir, but do not expect such a large settlement upon her. Do not expect my happiness in this marriage. Do not expect me to be your friend. Any of the advantages your wife sought to gain for you and your family through this marriage that I can deny to her, I shall. And neither she, nor her cruder daughters, shall ever be welcome at Pemberley or in my other houses, and you may tell Mrs. Bennet, and Elizabeth as well — nay *I* shall tell Elizabeth — that I will introduce the girls to *no* rich men, I shall toss them at none of my friends, and in fact I shall warn all my acquaintance against the Bennet girls. But I will do the duty my honor presents before me. I will marry your daughter. I will provide for your daughter. I will see to it that your grandchildren will be the heirs of one of the greatest estates in the land, and so, despite everything I might do, the dishonorable of this world have once more won."

Darcy had not expected to be taken by such passion. He fell silent. Still standing evenly balanced on both feet, though he now wanted to pace or sit down to relieve the stress in his ankle. He would not show any sign of discomfort.

He had nothing more to say.

Mr. Bennet's face showed he had nothing further to add in his turn.

Darcy nodded sharply. "Are matters between us settled?"

Mr. Bennet rose slowly, almost arthritically, though he could not yet be fifty from his appearance.

Darcy realized he did not want to shake his new *father's* hand, and he suspected from his appearance that Mr. Bennet did not wish to shake his hand. They would not part as though they were friends. Mr. Darcy inclined his head stiffly and fractionally once more. Mr. Bennet inclined his head a little deeper, and without a further word Darcy left the room.

*****

After Mr. Bennet heard the tale of the previous night from Elizabeth, when they were at last alone without Mrs. Bennet's screeching about how clever her daughter was, Mr. Bennet had been deeply unsettled and worried for Elizabeth.

That was before Mr. Darcy entered his study for the preceding interview.

He should act.

He should prevent this marriage.

Nothing to do. Nothing he *could* do. He was trapped into giving his consent as neatly as Mr. Darcy and Lizzy had been trapped by Mrs. Bennet and the other witnesses. If only, alas, *if only* they had not been seen.

He had questioned Lizzy at great length the previous night, and he understood what had happened. It had not crossed his mind before, as his perception had been blinded by the joking tale of Darcy loudly claiming that his Lizzy was not handsome enough to tempt him, but in retrospect the nature of the matter was obvious.

Though their characters were dissimilar and incompatible, an animal magnetism existed between his Lizzy and Mr. Darcy, stronger on Mr. Darcy's side, but the obsessed fascination had been present in Elizabeth as well. No *wonder* she talked so much, so gleefully about Wickham's likely ridiculous stories — *certainly* ridiculous stories.

The man who Wickham described would never have acted in the honorable way and made the offer to the poorly dowered girl he believed to have trapped him. Mr. Bennet had never believed that Mr. Darcy acted in a worse way than the average of very rich men. Now he believed Darcy was better than the average of rich men. That was something at least. Perhaps even a great deal.

He would not intentionally abuse her.

Lizzy had been fascinated by Mr. Darcy — for God's sake, what *stupidity* drew them to talk privately in the library. That was Darcy's fault; it was clear from the story. Elizabeth suggested the library, but Darcy suggested the private conference. And Lizzy said that Darcy had, after putting them both in such a delicate position for the chance to speak, told her no specifics, beyond that Wickham was an untrustworthy, unctuous seducer, which Mr. Bennet could see quite well enough without being told. Anyone could.

Except Lizzy, apparently.

She had angrily mentioned, as an aside, after describing how they had come to kiss, that she was yet resolved to think of Mr. Wickham as before, as Mr. Darcy had given no proof in his allegations against Wickham.

And that kiss, he understood it.

Two healthy young persons, alone in the candlelight.

A passionate animal magnetism between them, which they turned into sharp arguments. The blood boiled, the spirits rose, they were young, alive, full of energetic tension.

Lizzy tripped; Mr. Darcy caught.

Lizzy had admitted, not to Mrs. Bennet of course, but to Mr. Bennet, when they talked in his study while the first glimmers of dawn glimmered against the windows of his room, after he'd managed to put his wife and restless brood to bed, that she *had* chosen to kiss him as much as he had wished to kiss her.

They had stared into each other's eyes, full of emotion, and she had been wrapped around by the strong arms of a young man — a first time

— and she had leaned up her head to kiss him.

And just as she realized the wrongness of her position, and Mr. Darcy perhaps as well, the door had been thrown open, and they had been seen wrapped in each other's arms, passionately grabbing one another with Cupid's barbs.

Mr. Bennet saw no harm in the kiss itself. If the two had been left to their own devices they would have separated before they were entirely carried away by passion. Mr. Darcy, given his stiffness, would have disclaimed interest in Elizabeth, and probably, knowing his character, left the neighborhood the following day to put himself far from the temptation.

Or maybe they would have conversed upon it and decided they wished to marry due to passion, despite the dissimilarity in their characters. Mr. Bennet did not think Elizabeth was such a fool as to marry for the passion for a pretty face and form that had drawn him into his own marriage, but Mr. Darcy was decidedly rich, and he could provide even more benefits for her and the family than Mr. Bingley could, if Mr. Bingley offered for Jane.

After the spectacle of the last night, and with Darcy's promise to counsel his friends against marriage to the other Bennet daughters, Mr. Bennet thought there was a strong possibility that nothing would come of the attachment between Jane and Mr. Bingley.

Did a girl good to be jilted on occasion. Gave her distinction amongst her peers.

Mr. Bennet did not worry at all about Jane. It was Lizzy.

The worst possible situation — the mismatched couple, now despising the passion that was their only real link, since despite Mr. Darcy and Elizabeth both having quick, steady and clever minds, Mr. Bennet could see no real sympathy of the heart, spirit or mind betwixt them, no potential for that attachment mind to mind that he always wished to see for his beloved daughter, and which he thought Jane might find with Mr. Bingley. This mismatched, nay ill matched, couple were now forced to marriage, to the parson's mousetrap, and Mr. Darcy would despise his wife, falsely believing her to have been party to a low scheme to entrap him, and Elizabeth would be placed in the situation of being married to a man with no charm, no liveliness, no lightness of spirit. Further a man who despised whatever affection he did feel for her, and who thought her the lowest sort of woman.

Jove, Mr. Bennet rather wished Mr. Darcy had refused to make the offer out of righteous anger.

Mr. Bennet's insults to him had been subconsciously aimed to drive Mr. Darcy away, since in his conscious mind Mr. Bennet knew he had no choice: Scandal would wreck the whole family if the unhappy pair did not marry. He had failed to set aside any money for the maintenance of his children upon his passing, and thus one of the girls must marry well. And that would never happen if he drove Darcy away.

At the very least, he was sure that if he refused Darcy, the arrogant and angry man would definitely take Bingley with him, and that chance for Jane would be gone.

Poor, poor Lizzy. Trapped in such a situation.

Mr. Bennet's stomach ached when he imagined her stolen away from him — now with no permission to see her mother nor her sisters, though likely Darcy would relent on *that* matter, and with a husband whose passion would cool once slaked, and turn either into entire indifference or into tired hatred.

He only saw disgraceful ruin or the severest unhappiness for Elizabeth. And there was nothing he could do.

Chapter Three

Elizabeth woke early in the morning the day after the ball — far too early to wake up after a night where the dancing had continued almost till dawn.

The white paint on her ceiling stared back down at her. She was warm and cozy in bed, covered by several heavy quilts and with the carefully banked embers still glowing in the fireplace. It wasn't even cold today. Stay in bed... stay and never face the bizarre disaster last night had turned her life into.

Elizabeth wriggled back deeper into her bed and closed her eyes, and without intending to let her mind wander there, she relived the kiss. Her stomach shooting up into her throat as she fell. The way Darcy moved *so* fast, showing that all of his attention had been on her. His tight, warm grip around her hips, keeping her safe and secure. His smooth strong hands swinging her up to stand beside him.

His deep, intense *eyes*.

The sore sprain in her foot, forgotten. His lips on her lips, nibbling, caressing and pulling at her lips.

She had liked the kiss.

This ridiculous marriage could be worse. She could be being forced to marry a man whose mouth she hated.

All a terrible accident.

The rug's fault. Not her fault. Not Darcy's fault. The *rug's* fault. There, someone to blame who could not defend themselves. Once Jane married Bingley, she would make Mr. Bingley burn the rug. Or if he didn't want to destroy any furniture belonging to the house, she would make Bingley package it up and send it to the owner.

As forced and unwanted marriages went, hers was surprisingly promising. Darcy was a clever man. He said clever things about books. And society. He secretly made fun of Miss Bingley all the time, and Elizabeth did not like her either. And she liked talking to Darcy, however much she had pretended to despise his opinions. And there was a strong passion between them.

Elizabeth grinned, and, without really planning to get out of bed, she sat up, put her legs on the thick rug beneath her bed, stood and went to the wash basin to splash her face with cold water.

Whatever he had said when he first saw her, she *was* handsome enough to tempt him. And except when she wished to tease him, this would be the last time she would ever consider those first words to fall from his lips that she had heard. He liked her very well indeed — *that* was what all those dark silent looks which he had been sending her meant, they had been full of passion and admiration.

While Mr. Darcy was the last man in the world whom she would have chosen to marry, and while she would have sharply and angrily refused him if he had offered for her hand, now that the matter was a *fait accompli*, and now that she could *honorably* and *chastely* fantasize about kissing him once more, Elizabeth was not at all sure, on this morning following their interrupted interlude in Netherfield's library, that the situation which was leading to her marriage to Mr. Darcy was a bad matter about which she should mourn.

Elizabeth's hopeful mood lasted in full flower until he came to the drawing room from his closeted appointment with Mr. Bennet.

The two gentlemen announced that Mr. Darcy was to marry Elizabeth — that had been definitely decided on. Mrs. Bennet exclaimed, "The Lord has been very good to us! Oh, my *clever, clever* daughter."

Mr. Darcy bowed in reply every time Mrs. Bennet referred to him and he listened with ill concealed, at least to Elizabeth, impatience to Mrs. Bennet's effusive explanation of how she had always liked him, always thought the best of him, and never participated in the neighborhood's general dislike of Mr. Darcy.

"Men are so changeable — I knew, I always liked you. Even though the first thing you said — your very first words in Meryton had been that Lizzy was not handsome enough to tempt you." Mrs. Bennet laughed. "Oh! You were very tempted by my cleverest girl. Hertfordshire girls are the finest. Anyone will eventually succumb to our charm. Don't you worry — Lizzy can very well manage a house. You'll see. And you can see that she is very well raised. She'll be an excellent mother for your children. She has my example. She will be a mother just like me. You can see how well-mannered all of her children will be from how my children all behave, with the perfectest propriety and sweetness and good cheer no matter—"

"La!" Lydia shouted, bored by Mrs. Bennet's unending stream of words. "What a joke! Marrying terrible Mr. Darcy! It would have been more fun if Lizzy were to marry Mr. Collins, like he planned, but I suppose you shall do better as a brother. But I am *Wickham's* friend. I cannot believe Lizzy has forgotten our dear Mr. Wickham so easily as that. I shall not."

With a sniffing sneer, Lydia left the room.

Mr. Darcy coldly watched her go, and Elizabeth's stomach churned. He would despise her family so much that he would leave — except she knew Darcy would not do that. She somehow knew that abandoning her after kissing her in front of witnesses simply was not in his character. She somehow knew that she liked his character very much.

"As I was saying, all of my daughters are very well behaved, and Lizzy shall raise yours to be just as well behaved!"

Zounds! Every word from her mother made Mr. Darcy's face grew colder. Elizabeth did not want to see him so angry. She was not sure why. Only the day previous she had been sure she hated him. Now she wanted to protect him from her mother.

She desperately wanted him to approve of her.

"Mama!" Elizabeth exclaimed to silence her smilingly galloping mother. "Mr. Darcy wishes to speak, can you not see?"

"Oh, of course. I would never be one to speak over a gentleman, or prevent him from having the turn to make his opinions known, especially such a happy gentleman, whom I like so much as—"

"*Mama.*"

Mr. Darcy smiled, a little ironically at Elizabeth. "I would in truth like to have an opportunity to speak to my affianced with privacy."

Elizabeth's stomach leapt with butterflies.

Sharp clean shaven cheekbones. A finely tied cravat. Muscular shoulders which his riding coat clung to. He wanted her alone so he could kiss her again.

That must be his clever design.

She felt her face flush as she looked at him, and her heart raced.

Stop, Lizzy. He is too austere a man to just want a kiss. He wants to talk about practical matters around the engagement. And the like... And then he would kiss her again.

Mrs. Bennet winked at both of them, broadly. "Of course. Of *course*. Mr. Darcy." She tittered. "I shall leave you two *entirely* alone. I can *trust* you both without *chaperone*." She tittered again. "Lizzy! Such a clever girl."

Elizabeth flushed more completely, the red going down her neck and into her cleavage like the previous night. Her mother was embarrassing her. Again.

And with a shutting door they were alone.

Elizabeth demurely looked down at the floral sprigged pattern of their new rug. Mrs. Bennet declared shortly after they had bought the rug the previous year, while Mr. Bennet complained upon the price, that with this rug, even in the worst part of winter, they would have flowers in the drawing room.

Elizabeth could almost smell the red dyed roses.

Her heart beat fast, and her fingertips tingled.

Mr. Darcy said nothing.

He did not move. Elizabeth waited tensely. She secretly hoped he would stalk across the room and take her into his arms with one large embrace and kiss her intensely, like the previous night.

She would always remember falling into his arms like that.

He did not move.

Elizabeth looked up at Darcy. Part of her mind wanted her to stand stiffly and speak to him in a businesslike manner, showing that she was not presently ruled by the passion that had ruled them both the previous night.

Instead she looked up demurely through her eyelashes and smiled in what she hoped was a seductive manner. She bit her lower lip, like the heroine in a novel she had read recently constantly did.

Darcy groaned and looked away. "Do not look at me like that, madam."

"Like what?" Elizabeth said grinningly, now brave. She came closer to him, so close that she could smell his rich scent again. When he looked at her once more, she bit her lower lip once more. "What did you want us to *discourse* upon?"

He groaned again.

"Well, Mr. Darcy?" She grinned and leaned her head up towards him.

He shook himself and stepped away. But she could tell from how his eyes lingered on her lips, and occasionally dipped to her other attributes, that it was not an easy choice for him. "We must talk about practical matters. Yes. Practical matters."

"Of course." Elizabeth grinned, and bit her lip once more, enjoying the effect that gesture had on Mr. Darcy's attention. "Practical matters."

"Stop looking at me like that!" She had never seen him so flustered. "You'll not trick me again. You have so arranged that you have a rich husband. Your trap succeeded, but I shall not give you any great sum of pin money. You will receive the minimum suitable to your place as Mrs. Darcy."

Elizabeth gasped and stepped away, her hand flying to her mouth. All thought of seducing the still *odious* man fled. *She* had planned for them to be discovered? *He* had been the one to kiss her! Elizabeth spoke coldly. "I do not know what you are speaking of."

"Do not pretend to be innocent."

The harsh tone of his voice dampened, though it did not quench, the ardent fire that burned in Elizabeth's belly. "You *odious* man. You ungentlemanlike kisser and insulter of women. You think *I* trapped you!"

"Yes, Madam. You trapped me. It was no accident that right at the moment when we were kissing your mother opened the door with witnesses."

Elizabeth growled.

"Well?"

"You are being ridiculous. It was a coincidence."

"Just admit the truth. You intended to use my passion for you to trap me into marriage."

"Passion? I had no idea you had the slightest attachment to me before last night. You *had* once claimed me to be too unhandsome to tempt you."

"You should not listen to the conversations of other people."

"And you should not have sneeringly insulted on a public dance floor the entirety of *my* neighborhood. And then kissed me."

Elizabeth threw back the accusation.

She panted. Like she had when she angrily argued with Darcy last night. *Odious,* odious man. He was wrong. *So* wrong. With such fine thin lips. She wanted to shout at him and kiss him at the same time. Hopefully he was feeling the same thing. The kissing part at least.

He was.

She could *now* read that dark look in his eyes. And then he seemed to actually hear what she had accused him of at last and he grimaced. "Yes. Last night was not the only failure of my honor and self-control. I ought to have made a better pretence of politeness to the neighborhood. I was wrong to fail in that."

"You shouldn't have thought you were above us at all."

"I am above your neighborhood. You now shall be above them too. I shall expect you also to behave as though you are above them once we marry. You should keep distance from those who are no longer worthy of your attention, and—"

"What? You want me to treat my *neighbors,* the people I have grown up with, as though they are—"

"As though they are of little consequence in the world. Which they are. You can shower them with condescension, but—"

"Lord! If I wanted to listen to *this,* I would have married Mr. Collins."

That silenced him. Good. Odious man. She didn't even want to kiss him again anymore.

Yes, yes you do.

Darcy stepped closer to her. So close she could smell his cologne and the spicy scent of his breath. He was big and well proportioned, and she loved... uh admired... uh lustfully beheld his Grecian (whatever *that* meant, but it sounded decidedly handsome) profile, and his strong chin.

"Elizabeth — we can call each other by our Christian names as we are to marry. I just want..."

His breath caught. Her breath caught.

Their faces were only inches apart, and they felt closer. She could just reach her hand forward and touch his lips. She could just lean her face up, and he could just lower his lips to hers and kiss her.

Please.

"Elizabeth." He took a deep steadying breath, though the arousal in his dark eyes remained. "I just want you to admit to me you know it was wrong to entrap me in this way."

"Zounds! You lumbering, lurching oaf!" Elizabeth tried to push him away with her hands, but she just pushed herself instead of pushing both of them. "I didn't trap you! You — you — you trapped *me*!"

Darcy raised one eyebrow briefly in skepticism.

"*Think*. I could not have planned for my mother to enter at the moment when *you* kissed me."

"You kept a count in your head, waiting for the right moment, so that there would be enough time for us to be thoroughly engrossed in the kiss, but insufficient time for me to remember my position and push you away, and your mother brought the witnesses together, keeping the same count."

"We were in the library for ten minutes! You cannot *imagine* that my mother could keep a consistent time count for so long."

He raised that single eyebrow again.

"I *tripped*! You were the brute who kissed me."

"You certainly kissed me in return. Do not pretend you didn't enjoy it."

Elizabeth paused, clenching and unclenching her fists like claws.

Oh, if only she could scream to him about how he was taking advantage of a poor helpless maiden who had no knowledge of congress between men and women, and who certainly had not wanted any such kiss, nor participated willingly in their kiss. And who definitely did not enjoy any part of that kiss.

Alas, her mother had taught her not to lie.

"I can too," Elizabeth said at last, with an air of wounded dignity, "pretend that I did not enjoy it. And I always shall — do not expect me to confess that truth. And I did *not* seek your kiss."

"Madam, I understand your choosing to entrap me in this way. You saw my attraction—"

She sneered. "Ridiculous!"

Darcy didn't have any attraction for her, and he was just pretending to claim he did, to make his kissing her sound less horrible. Elizabeth really had no notion why the strange man was saying he had been attracted. She would never be able to understand him, not even if she had fifty years to study his character.

Which you will.

No. No. No. Not such unpleasant thoughts. He would probably die after only forty more years.

Elizabeth shuddered, uncomforted by her attempt to comfort herself.

Better to think about pleasant things. Darcy supposedly had a gigantesque house with superb grounds, and she'd have several carriages and a great deal of dresses. *That* is what she should think on, since she was never to marry for love.

Fah! Love! Who needs it?

At least as many poets decried the feeling, and called it madness, insane, not worth the bother, et cetera, as praised the emotion. She could do very well without any love in her life.

"You saw my attraction," Darcy said again, "and as you did not wish to be made to marry Mr. Collins by your mother— " Elizabeth yet another time snorted and sneered. "You offered her an alternative, by entrapping me."

"I would have refused Mr. Collins — this assumes he meant to ask me — and Papa would have supported me. I am by no means persuaded Mr. Collins would have made the offer... He must recognize how ill suited we are."

Mr. Darcy pressed his fine pale lips together into a thin smile, and he raised just one eyebrow, again. The picture of skepticism.

"How do you do that?" Elizabeth asked as she compulsively raised both of her eyebrows several times. "I want to respond with the same skeptical single eyebrow, but it is not working."

Was that a smile? Mr. Darcy kept the one eyebrow up, firmly, but his lips *definitely* were smiling.

He could be excessively handsome when he smiled. Even if he *did* think she had *wanted* to end up in this situation.

"Come now! Reveal the secret. Unless it was something taught in one of those exclusive male clubs where they made you to all bow in togas before a collection of skulls stolen from a museum of medical curiosities before swearing to never share the secret."

"What?"

"Come now, Mr. Darcy — everyone knows that young aristocrats of your sort—"

"I am untitled."

"Aristocratic youths then, of your sort, join the most absurd dining clubs when in university. And that you rule the world with these cabals that determine the next prime minister, the outcome of the wars, and whether or not good Christianity will be outlawed by the Masons. And how to raise one eyebrow at a time."

"Oh! *Those* clubs. Yes, well, I did not learn the secret there, so I am under no oath to hide the trick from you. But unfortunately, I do not *know* how I do it. It was a habit of my father's. I must have simply imitated him as a child, and thus gained the skill. Perhaps if you practice in a mirror..."

Elizabeth threw her hands up. "Useless. I am to get an unexpected and unsought — I did not trap you — husband, with the most remarkable and unusual skill, and I gain no benefit from it."

Mr. Darcy looked at her again, with one skeptical eyebrow raised.

Men. Useless.

That smile playing on the edge of his lips was quite handsome. Maybe she should look on the bright sunny side of matters if she was going to be forced to marry this man. Specifically she should look at that smile.

If she could get him to smile like that all the time... she could very well bear being his wife.

"Come, Mr. Darcy." Elizabeth smiled. "We are to marry. We should make the best of it. I am now convinced there will be some excellent aspects to this."

His smile collapsed. "You mean Pemberley."

"No! I mean your smile and the kiss we—" Elizabeth's face flushed. God she could not believe she just shouted that. And Mama was probably hiding on the other side of the door, with her ear to the keyhole, listening to every word they said.

"It takes more than animal passions to make a good relationship. You lack entirely in connections, and wealth, and morality. I just wish you to admit that you—"

"I did not seek to entrap you."

"You did."

Their faces hovered inches in front of each other once more.

And once more the two of them kissed. Lips desperately pressing together, tongues, and gripping of clothes and bodies.

When they paused for breath, Elizabeth added once more, "Did not."

Darcy kissed her once more in reply.

Chapter Four

Darcy was treated to a cold dinner by Miss Bingley when he returned bruised-lipped to Netherfield from his morning kissing call at Longbourn.

Deuced thing with Bingley gone up to London for the next days, was that he was left with his friend's sister who was determined to take the whole matter of Darcy marrying Miss Elizabeth *very* personally. Not as though he ever had any intention of marrying *her* no matter how many young ladies of distinction Miss Bingley could Christian name because they also attended that *reportedly* fine school Bingley's tradesman progenitor sent her and Mrs. Hurst to.

Miss Bingley glared at Darcy from the far side of the food laden dinner table as if he had sinned against her and God.

If Darcy had been found alone in a room with Miss Bingley...

He certainly would never have kissed her. So they would have been found chastely speaking if such a thing *had* happened. So there would have been no call for them to marry.

The silence was as cold as the food, and her frosty gaze stopped any attempt for anyone else to speak. The cook had set the leftover meats from the previous night's feast out in the cellar, kept almost freezing by the late November air, and Miss Bingley was feeding them back to her party of guests without having allowed Cook to reheat the meat or fat congealed soup.

A symbolic way of showing her displeasure towards him.

Like Darcy cared.

The plates clinked as the footmen ladled cold soup into the bowls, and Darcy grabbed with the large serving fork a healthy heap of cold roast beef and mutton. There was ample freshly baked, still warm from the oven, breads, and cold gravy to dip it in.

He actually liked the taste of finally salted and seasoned meat when it was cold and a day old.

"I would not have left bed," Mr. Hurst peevishly said, "if I had known we would eat the same food as last night." He waved to the footman standing behind them. "Go to the kitchen, and get Cook to prepare a ragout — a decent one. Not like that last. And quick about it. I expect something more than cold meat! This is my brother's house, and he'd be quite disappointed at how I'm being served in his absence."

Miss Bingley rolled her eyes. "I told Cook to not make more food. This is ample for our *guest*." She sharply looked at Darcy, with that orange sour lemon expression she liked.

Darcy laughingly thought to himself: *Ah, the guest. And yesterday I had been family.*

It would be rude to say it aloud.

"I'm also your guest," Mr. Hurst protested. "Besides, Bingley put you no more in charge of the kitchens than Louisa."

Darcy happily chewed a charred piece of lamb. If Miss Bingley hoped to annoy him with the simple fare, she would be gravely disappointed.

Miss Bingley muttered to Mrs. Hurst so low that Darcy was quite sure she did not want him to hear — the first words from any of the four at the table, except Mr. Hurst's complaints at the quality of the meal — "in *my* library. Scorning me in *my* library."

Who, Darcy wondered, had scorned her? Himself or Elizabeth? Also, *Bingley's* library.

Mrs. Hurst also glared at Darcy.

"Ha! You really are put out by Darcy marrying a prettier girl than you."
Mr. Hurst paused, a bite halfway to his mouth. He spoke to Darcy,
"Reminds me, that does. Haven't congratulated you yet. Miss Elizabeth.
Fine girl. Fine. The two of you are well matched. You have no need of
any dowry." He laughed, and took what remained of the bite after
several drops of the gravy had splattered the white silk table cloth. "Not
like me and Louisa."

"I thank you for the congratulations." Darcy then added, for Miss
Bingley's benefit, "I truly am coming to believe that the constant
hunting for the best dowry, and the need to ensure that your partner is
the best in status that you can achieve is a cause of great misery, and
much immorality and scheming, and many behaviors which we would
not wish to admit to before religion."

Mr. Hurst swallowed his meat down with the help of half his glass of
wine. "Well said! Darcy, well said." He raised his glass high, nearly
sloshing the liquid over the sides. "To marriages of affection."

Darcy raised his glass in return, and they clinked, while the two sisters
blank faced stared at the gentlemen.

"To marriages of affection," Darcy repeated.

Was he actually entering a marriage of affection?

"The worst of it," Mr. Hurst added as he motioned a footman to refill his
glass of wine, "is when ridiculous disappointed hopes lead to a cold
dinner. There is *never* a good reason for a cold leftover dinner."

Miss Bingley hissed at her brother-in-law. "Those scheming women. I
am sure Darcy did not mean to ask Miss Elizabeth to marry him. You do
not need to, you do not need to go through with this! Not if you do not
wish to. It was a compromising situation she devised. A sign of
immorality. She shall be the mother of your children, and their
grandmother shall be Mrs. Bennet."

Mr. Hurst laughed. "I dare say Darcy wants Miss Elizabeth full much. Be a fool not to. With her fine, fine..." Mr. Hurst trailed off as Darcy stared with his best intimidating mask at him. Darcy would not listen to Elizabeth's charms being crudely bantered about, not by anyone. "Uh, her mind. Her fine mind... They are both great readers. It was singular how she preferred reading to cards. Singular. Much like Darcy. Don't be a sour Caro."

"So you approve?" Darcy tilted his head.

"Course I do. A surprise, but shows your good sense. Course I approve. You heard Bingley's congratulations. *Everyone* heard Bingley's congratulations."

Yes. Bingley's congratulations. Everyone *had* heard Bingley's congratulations.

Why did it have to be *Bingley* there to see him kissing Elizabeth? Perhaps if it had just been Lizzy's neighbors he could have pretended the whole thing never happened. At least to himself. He would still have needed to ask Elizabeth to marry him, but he would have been able to pretend it didn't happen, anyways. But his closest friend had seen him in that moment of ungentlemanly behavior and passion.

And then congratulated him.

Miss Bingley said bitterly, "You can well imagine how *she* shall set up camp at Pemberley, always needing to live with her dear daughter, and she will foist her girls on every friend you have, and she will presume on your credit in town, and when they see her vulgar manner, her loudness, and the behavior of your *sisters*, your good name will be quite ruined. All because that *scheming*—"

"Do not insult my betrothed."

Miss Bingley gripped her knife so hard her knuckles turned white. It was fortunate that Elizabeth was *not* present at the table, as she might be in some danger from Sour Caro. He would tell her about how sour Miss Bingley looked when she was faced with the final fact that he would never marry her.

Elizabeth would laugh at the story.

Strange that he wanted to tell Elizabeth about everything suddenly.

But he did. And he liked that he did.

"Are you going to let Mrs. Bennet ruin you?"

Mr. Hurst laughed. "Caro, you *are* a sour cherry, aren't you."

"I do not intend to allow Mrs. Bennet to ruin anything," Darcy replied. "And I am determined to treat my future family with exactly the respect they deserve."

He stared Miss Bingley down. She looked away and tightened her jaw.

Darcy sawed off another piece from the joint of roast meat. A fine rich gravy, all the better for being cold and fat soaked.

"She doesn't love you. Just your money."

Darcy raised one eyebrow.

"She doesn't," Miss Bingley insisted.

"I am quite certain that Miss Elizabeth has a great deal of admiration and affection for my person," Darcy replied smugly.

Mr. Hurst said, "Hear! Hear! Noble mien. Tall form. Athletic active figure. Any girl would want you."

Darcy looked at Mr. Hurst like he were a puzzle he could not quite solve. Was Hurst making fun of him?

Mr. Hurst amiably smiled and forked another dripping chunk of beef into his wide maw. He brushed his lips with the cotton edge of his napkin.

Elizabeth may have kissed Darcy to entrap him, but kissing him had *not* been an unpleasant duty for her, and the kisses this morning were entirely because she *wanted* to kiss him, even though she was angry at his refusal to accept her pretence of innocence.

A line from Lear crossed Darcy's mind, and he reworded the Bard's phrase to fit the situation: His Lady was fair, and there would be good sport at the making of their children.

Elizabeth was a passionate woman with clinging lips and fingers. He understood exactly why Hurst congratulated him, and Mr. Hurst did not even know the half of it. In truth Darcy did not yet either. But he would. He would explore every feature of Elizabeth, and he would touch every part of her, and when they were married, he would not let her leave his bed for — "Eh, what did you say about Miss Jane?"

"I said," Miss Bingley repeated with exasperation, "that no matter what you think about Miss Elizabeth, you cannot want my brother to also be trapped by one of these Bennet girls. I could not stand to see their schemes succeeding so thoroughly that they trap two of the finest gentlemen in the land. One compromised man is quite enough. You must do something to save Bingley from Miss Jane."

Mr. Hurst pushed his plate away and signalled the footman to take it away. He sighed gustily. "Surprisingly good, though cold. Caro, it's Bingley's place to decide. Connection with Darcy's *sister* would be worth the loss of dowry."

Miss Bingley hissed at him. "Must you be obtuse?"

Darcy remembered the ball the day before. He had closely observed Miss Jane the previous night, and determined that she had no real liking for Bingley. He had planned to warn his friend away from the woman.

His conversation with Elizabeth in the library, and its results had driven all such thoughts from his mind. "You also think Bingley would marry Miss Bennet?"

"His angel! You know how he is. He would forget about her in a week if we made him stay in London. We should all go, we could leave and be safe from any gossip, and tell our friends that it is all lies and—"

"Miss Bingley. I do not know how to make this clearer: I am going to marry Miss Elizabeth Bennet. I will hear no further words against my choice from you."

"You should marry someone with the education and fortune you expect... someone who is a friend. Who cares for *you*. It hurts me to see you taken in and trapped by such a—"

"That was the last time. Further, Miss Bingley, is seems I must speak plainly to you, as hints, and even my engagement, does not seem to be enough to make you understand: you had some hope, I see — though I never gave you anything which could be construed as particular encouragement — that I might choose to marry you. Never did any possibility, not the most miniscule, of such an offer exist. My marriage to Elizabeth is completely irrelevant to what hopes you may have had, as they were entirely misplaced from the outset."

Miss Bingley looked like a puppy that had been kicked. Darcy felt a little guilty.

Half his silver plate of food still sat before him, filled with tasty meat. Darcy had been hungry but now he could not take another bite. He did not like hurting anyone, not even Miss Bingley.

Mr. Hurst said loudly, "I wonder when my ragout shall arrive?"

Darcy stood. "I am taking a ride — when Bingley does return, I will counsel him to be in no hurry, and to be sure of his feelings and of her feelings before he makes any offer to Miss Bennet. My observation showed that Miss Bennet has no particular liking for your brother, and I shall tell him that."

She nodded silently, without looking up at him. Miss Bingley pale facedly stirred the dregs of her white soup around and around.

Darcy would also tell Mr. Bingley to make sure he never found himself alone in a room with Miss Bennet. Just in case. From her appearance he did not think Jane would stoop to such low tricks as kissing him while witnesses waited to spring upon them.

He also had not thought Elizabeth would stoop to such a low trick either.

*****

Darcy took a furious ride that led him ten miles from Netherfield towards London. He stopped when he had rode the horse up to the top of a high sloping hill, and he dismounted at the cold ridge. From here, facing London, it was possible to see in the distance in the cold clear air the smudge of the fog and the curving of the Thames. The individual buildings were no more distinguishable from almost twenty miles distance than the leaves on a tree a thousand feet away were.

Darcy walked Marcus Aurelius, his big stallion, for ten minutes to let the horse calm down from its race before hobbling him in the middle of some rough grasses that the weather had left, and pouring out a small pile of oats for him to snack on.

He always had packed in his saddle bag a tightly stoppered bottle of ink, a neatly cut pen and a pen knife, and a dozen folded sheets of fine writing paper with a hard back to set them against, in case he had occasion to write a letter whilst upon the road.

Darcy took these implements from the bag and sat against a tree trunk.

The afternoon sun warmed him.

A pleasant day, despite the season. The sticks of the trees were pretty in the cold clear air. The air was cold enough that after he stripped off his right glove to write, his hand began to go numb, but the day was yet warm enough that he could easily write for a half hour.

He needed to tell those closest to him about the marriage, especially since Mr. Collins would tell Lady Catherine as soon as he returned to Hunsford. He did not want the clergyman to be the one to inform his aunt and cousin — they deserved better warning than that — and he did not want the rest of the family to learn about Elizabeth from Lady Catherine's rants.

Darcy wrote his first letter to his cousin, Colonel Fitzwilliam. In addition to Georgiana's guardianship the two gentlemen shared a deep friendship and confidence. There was no one else to whom Darcy would turn for advice on a matter near to his heart, and about which he yet felt a great uneasiness.

I expect my news shall surprise you exceedingly, and I hope this news shall please you some. Except I cannot say for myself whether I am deeply pleased or made entirely miserable. In a word: I have found myself obliged to marry a woman of no fortune, no connections, no family, and little breeding — no that is not true, her manners are perfect, though not those of high society. And I have ended up in this situation through my own lack of discipline, through a passionate failure of control which was quite contrary to my normal habits. But it was her scheming stratagem which made it such that my failure of perfect self-reserve led to our necessity to marry.

Darcy hurriedly scribbled, carefully blotting out each line, to keep the ink from messing his pants. He'd built up a little berm of cold dirt around the inkpot to keep it stable, and he carefully kept from knocking it over each time he dipped the quill in. He had written several times before while sitting outside, and it always was a freeing sensation, to do such an indoors activity whilst looking at nature. Almost as if he were a romantic poet like a Wordsworth or a Coleridge, instead of a steady and sober English gentleman of consequence.

He told Colonel Fitzwilliam the tale: Elizabeth tripping — he would have sworn then that she had truly tripped over the bear's head. Her fall had *appeared* unintentional. And her eyes. She had been as surprised as he at the feeling in both of their eyes that required he kiss her. At the moment she fell into his arms, he would have sworn her reactions were natural and innocent.

She had been truly passionate. And her anger towards him about Wickham's story? Had that been feigned? Only a strange sort of woman would pretend anger towards a man who she hoped to entrap in marriage.

His understanding of the situation made no sense.

Darcy ground his teeth together.

She had. She had trapped him. And happy as he was — Darcy blinked in shock as the surprise went through his mind. Not happy. He shouldn't say to himself that he was happy. He was unhappy.

Of *course* he was unhappy.

He was *supposed* to be unhappy. So he would be unhappy. Even if he felt happy.

He was marrying a woman with, as he wrote, no fortune, no connections, and an unpleasant family.

Darcy was chilled and stiff when he finished writing the story.

He had sat on the rocky ground without moving for a half hour, and part of the root of the tree had dug through his riding breeches until it painfully bit into his thigh. Darcy stood, and he hid his right hand inside his coat, pressing the half frozen fingers against the warm skin of his chest. He enjoyed the partly painful tingles as sensation and warmth returned to his digits.

He put the letter and his writing supplies back in the saddle bag with his left hand. His hobbled horse, Marcus Aurelius, placidly stood near the tree. Darcy pulled out an apple and a carrot from his bag. He took a bite from the apple, and as he chewed it he fed the carrot to his fine stallion, whose lips softly flapped over Darcy's hand as the animal quickly munched away the vegetable.

The stallion poked its nose towards the apple, and sniffed at it as Darcy held the apple away. Darcy scratched between Marcus's eyes and took another juicy bite from his apple before feeding it to the big brown horse.

The horse seemed to smile happily as he finished the apple, core and all, in three big bites.

Darcy walked back and forth over the ridge he'd stopped on. The light was fading, and the sun in the west lit the clouds brilliant oranges and yellows. London was in the far distance, still another two hours ride away, while it was an hour back to Netherfield, and that only if he rode half the distance at a canter.

It was time to start back if he wanted to be back at the estate in good time.

When Darcy returned to Netherfield, before he bathed and changed for supper, he sat down for an extra ten minutes to finish his letter to Colonel Fitzwilliam:

I solely want one *thing. Merely* one *thing from her, and then we can happily plan and discuss how we shall live — for I believe that the two of us shall get on well together, and I have become more convinced the more I think upon it that in person and temperament we shall fit excellently. Had she fortune and family, I would have offered for Miss Elizabeth without any need for such encouragement.*

I am no longer so unhappy about her mother and her sisters, nor even her relations in trade, relations who I shall require her to weaken the connection with to the greatest extent compatible with proper family feeling. I am to marry her. It will be her kisses I wake up to, not her mother's dull witted complaining.

I am committed to ensuring that the Bennet family profits as little as possible from their successful scheme. I have agreed to marry her, and so I shall. But the settlement will give Elizabeth nothing beyond a minimum of security. There will be enough pin money for necessities — I am no barbarian, and if she practices economy, she shall be able to purchase all accoutrements needed for a woman of Mrs. Darcy's stature, and ample other luxuries, but I shall put nothing towards her beyond a few hundred pounds per annum. Anything else she wishes, she shall need to tell me of the desire.

My understanding from discussions within the neighborhood is that Mr. Bennet has impoverished himself by always accepting his wife's demands to spend. And to spend. And to spend again, on ridiculous matters, when they should accumulate dowries for their daughters, like reasonable parents faced with an entail. Even were he to have a son, it would be a crime against future generations to break the entail, as Mr. Bennet no doubt intended to, so that the girls might have dowries.

They should set money aside.

If Miss Elizabeth expects me to be manipulated into spending upon her every whim in the manner that Mr. Bennet is by his wife, she shall be greatly disappointed.

But that is not a matter of importance. We are sensible adults. Both of us. We can discuss and agree reasonably upon matters of spending.

The one *thing I want, before I can be happy in this marriage, is that she admit the truth. I am an honest and forthright man. I despise deception. I want her to simply say that she meant to use my passion to trap me in marriage. To admit that it was a stratagem.*

That is all I want.

Your captured cousin,

F Darcy

Chapter Five

Elizabeth set off the next morning along the road into Meryton with Jane — she could not stand the company of any of her other sisters in the present crisis. They did not have any sense of the awfulness of her position.

She was entirely roiled inside, and unable to settle upon whether to be *really* unhappy or *moderately* happy about her sudden, unwanted engagement to an arrogant man of deep passions and tall noble features. A man who was convinced she had connived and cunningly used low and illegitimate arts to bring him to the point where he had no choice but to marry her, which, as Elizabeth angrily reminded herself, she *had not*.

Tripped. She had tripped.

Tripped, not trapped.

Tripped into his strong, muscular wrapping arms.

Mmmmmmmmm.

Strong arms.

Bad thought, Lizzy. Very unchaste.

If she was going to marry such a disdainful and arrogant man, who was completely certain in himself, Elizabeth should feel free to take pleasure in the one great inducement to matrimony she had.

No, *not* the pin money. Or Pemberley's exceptional library. Or the grounds which were reputed the finest in Derbyshire.

Darcy's appearance. He was *extremely* fine looking. Fine, fine, fine.

So it was in a state of roiled, aroused nerves that Elizabeth intended this morning to participate in that time honored soothing ritual: shopping.

Her preferred form of self-soothing behavior was through the purchase of books. Mr. Hyde, the bookseller, would do well today, as she intended to buy at *least* four new books — and Mama had given her extra money for her allowance, as she was so pleased with Elizabeth's success in catching such a rich gentleman.

It was a sign of her proper modesty to prefer reading to purchasing ornate objects of self-serving decoration.

Alas, Elizabeth sighed at the thought, this claim of disinterest in her outer appearance was not particularly true. Certainly she was not obsessed with self adornment, but to any person of a Puritanical and excessively religious nature, she would need to make confession that she liked fine silk dresses, flowers in her hair, and jewelry around her wrists and neck at least as much as the next lady.

Probably more, since everything looked better on her than on most women.

Elizabeth could happily admit to herself that she was handsomer than almost any woman she was acquainted with, even if Jane's presence was a constant reminder that there were echelons of beauty and charm, and angelic perfection which she could not hope to do more than touch.

And she could only touch those realms of perfect beauty by touching Jane, who did inhabit them.

No, her present disinclination to purchase objects of ornamentation came from less exalted motives: Mama had spent the entire night crowing about what expensive dresses and pin money that Elizabeth would have.

The whole night.

That was the real reason Elizabeth was only buying books instead of also purchasing a pretty ribbon or a new bonnet.

She had been unable to sleep a wink due to the enthusiastic, endless conjectures on which of the famous dressmakers, who were presently just names, and perhaps a street direction in London, that this odd creature, about to be birthed unwanted upon the world, Mrs. Darcy would choose to patronize. And the energetic exclamations on how fine the silk she would wear would be, and on how Elizabeth would have a separate dress for every day of the month once her wardrobe was complete.

Elizabeth at present seriously contemplated taking an oath that after her marriage she would only wear sackcloth and ashes for at least a six-month.

And those thin silk nightdresses Mrs. Gardiner once told her about that women wore to entice the lust of their husbands...

With *that* thought in mind, Elizabeth and Jane Bennet met upon the road to Meryton a gentleman who was charming, personable, and entirely inferior to Mr. Darcy in terms of masculine magnetism *and* distinguished nobility of appearance and haughtiness of manner. Her erstwhile almost friend, Mr. Wickham.

It was a strange feeling. Since her soon-husband despised Mr. Wickham, Elizabeth was conscious of a sense that she *ought* to avoid the gentleman, and treat him coldly in the way Mr. Darcy would. But at the same time, she had not chosen to marry Mr. Darcy, and to take up his interests, and perhaps she *could* help Wickham, though she much doubted Darcy would ever hear a word for him.

Darcy had claimed Wickham was a seducer of women.

The ingratiating smirk upon his face when he met the ladies suggested that there might be *something* to the charge. "Miss Elizabeth, and Miss Bennet. What happy chance for me to fall upon your company."

Jane smiled and curtsied. "We are walking to the bookstore."

"Not to shop for clothes, but then, Miss Elizabeth, I understand you are to have *ample* opportunity to shop at the *best* and I do understand that you do not wish to duplicate the effort now since *soon* you will shop at great length in London."

Elizabeth flushed. "I have heard enough of this from my mother."

He laughed gaily. "I salute you — I hear it was a quite clever scheme you played on him. Quite clever. To think that you found his *manner* repellent only a seven day past — I even thought you might have some favor towards a poor officer of the militia. But alas, it seems the *fortune* of one repellent is of greater attractiveness than the ample attractions of the fortuneless."

Jane frowned at Wickham. "Surely you are not suggesting my sister solely is marrying Mr. Darcy for his money."

"Solely for his money?" Wickham grinned delightedly. "I myself have described to her the beauties of Pemberley — the finest estate in the country, I dare say. That is a gem beyond price, as Darcy shall never sell it. *I* would marry Darcy to live high at Pemberley again."

"Lizzy and Darcy are not—" Jane paused, not at all sure what to say. Elizabeth had made her anxious sister privy to everything which happened, and she conveyed as strongly as she could the strength of her lustful inclinations towards Darcy to Jane (though she tried to make them sound *less* lustful for Jane), to assuage her sister's worries. "Lizzy has a definite admiration for Darcy."

Wickham winked at her. "Well played, Miss Bennet. He has many admirable assets, kept protected in his safebox and wallet. Though a sense of honor is not among them."

Whatever his faults, Darcy was a completely, perhaps excessively, honorable man. Elizabeth growled at Wickham. "You wrong him. I understand his character better now, and I assure you it is not for his fortune—"

"And to compromise him. That must have been hard to time with your mother. And a great risk — how did you convince him into the room alone with you?"

"What nonsense are you nattering about?"

"Fitzwilliam Darcy. He always sneered and pretended to be better than everyone, and completely made of cold, hard iron — but the iron was cast wrong and brittle! Hahahahaha."

"What are you talking about?"

"I never would have imagined that your *love creature* would be foiled in his intentions to only marry the most distinguished and well-dowered woman by the schemes of a woman such as you." Wickham bowed elaborately. "I salute you, Miss Elizabeth. I judged you made of softer stuff than this."

"I *tripped!*" Why had she ever thought this man was charming? Why had she ever felt any sense of connection to him?

"You *tripped*. And that is how you were found kissing?" He raised one eyebrow skeptically, like Darcy had the previous day.

"I swear, I was not trying to entrap him into marrying me."

Wickham laughed again. "It was how well-*endowed* you are." He gestured crudely at her breasts. "I see how your *endowment* tempted him away from Miss de Bourgh's endowment — but if you'd not been seen like that, he would have walked away from your *endowment*." Wickham leeringly and unashamedly eyeballed her breasts.

Jane gasped and looked honestly shocked. Elizabeth was by now quite prepared to expect anything from Wickham. Darcy had been entirely right about him.

"I will simply say once," Elizabeth glared at him, "and after that we shall part, for as my betrothed is at odds with you, it is not my place to engage in conversation with you, *I did not plan to be seen like that.*"

Mr. Wickham raised one eyebrow skeptically, again.

Elizabeth really hated that look. He must have learned it the same way Darcy did, by imitating Mr. Darcy's father. She hated it *more* than when Darcy did it, because underneath her anger at Darcy, and her dislike of his manners and arrogance, she actually liked Mr. Darcy. And now she was realizing that underneath her like for Mr. Wickham's appearance and charming manners and easy conversation, she despised him.

Wickham laughed when Elizabeth took Jane's arm and began to walk away towards Mr. Hyde's bookshop. "A week ago today we agreed that he *was* a dishonorable man — confess, did I give you courage to spring your trap upon him? When you learned that he deserved it after what he did to my position following my dear Godfather's death?"

"Had I intended to entrap him," Elizabeth sneered in response, "I would rather have taken your story as a warning against such a risky stratagem, as I would then believe him to be entirely without honor. Which I now know he is not. I think I always knew he was, in truth, honorable. Unlike you."

Wickham's face fell into an ugly snarl.

"Wickham!"

Darcy rode up the road from Netherfield, at a gallop, as though he intended to run Wickham over. The officer sneered at his childhood friend, puffing out his red coated chest with the white belts crossing in the middle, but when Darcy did not slow his horse, and the well-trained animal seemed to show no inclination to avoid trampling Wickham, he flinched and jumped out of the way, away from Elizabeth.

"Miss Elizabeth. Elizabeth," Darcy said, affecting to ignore Wickham, though he still stood five feet away. "I would kindly ask you, as my future wife, to never have any conversation with that man again."

And there was the arrogance again.

Why had she ever thought she liked the odious man at all?

"You are remarkably high-handed and commanding. And you still give no cogent proof for why I should dislike him. If I am to believe his story" — Elizabeth realized as she spoke she did not believe it any longer — "he has been wronged horribly by you."

Elizabeth then flushed and looked down. She should not argue with Darcy just to be contrary, just because she was annoyed at the way he asked her to not do what she had already decided to never do again. She should not argue with him in public at all.

"Lies!" Darcy glowered furiously at Wickham and leapt from his big black horse. "What *lies* have you spoken of me?"

Wickham blanched, bowed slightly and inarticulately to Jane and Elizabeth, and fled up the road without saying a word to Darcy.

She should be horrified by the raw violence present in Darcy's manner. He was probably on the verge of calling Wickham out for a duel.

Which would be bad.

Very bad. Elizabeth reminded herself firmly that she disapproved of duels entirely.

Why then did she feel alive, with the blood rushing to her toes and fingers, and tingles and flutters all over at seeing Darcy's upright head, clenched fists, and coiled posture. He was prepared to physically attack the fleeing Wickham.

She never imagined before two nights ago that the excessively fastidious Darcy had a passionate temper. He looked like a lion ready to roar in defense of its mate and its prey.

He looked her over as if she were both.

Elizabeth shivered and helplessly bit her lip. Her breasts felt full, and she wanted his touch again.

"Madam," Darcy swallowed. His eyes were dark and wide with a look as though he were about to grab her, throw her over his back, and carry her off to his lair, like a Highlander highwayman. He slowly reached his hand up to brush her cheek.

With a cough Jane shuffled her feet and said, "Poor Wickham. But it was excessively shocking what he said about Lizzy. Abominably improper. But poor man, to not have been taught better manners. If only he knew that one should not say such things to a lady. He looks more cultured than he is."

Darcy barked out a harsh laugh. He said to Elizabeth, still looking at her like she was something he'd chased down and leapt upon, like a lion leaping on its prey, "We have yet to complete our conversation upon Wickham, but I would have you to swear to never speak to him again."

Rather than indignation at the demand, Elizabeth felt liquid fire pooling in her belly at the look in his wide eyes.

*****

The three of them went to Longbourn, for Elizabeth's plan to call at the bookstore was paused when Darcy insisted on returning with her home so that he could speak to Mr. Bennet on Wickham's failings.

Darcy closeted himself with Mr. Bennet, and he revealed to the subdued gentleman several stories of how Wickham had treated those amongst the lower classes.

When he was done speaking about the danger Mr. Wickham represented, Mr. Bennet sighed, and like he had the previous day, he pulled his spectacles from his nose and wiped them off with a white cloth from his desk. Darcy thought it might be a nervous habit.

"You are worried that Elizabeth likes Mr. Wickham too much."

Darcy thinned his lips. "Should I not be? She has repeatedly defended his character to me."

"I can't tell. I simply can't tell." Mr. Bennet put his spectacles back on and peered at Darcy.

"Are you being intentionally mysterious? I simply demand to know whether you will listen to my warning and do at last something to protect the respectability of your family, and the condition of your daughters and gentlewomen."

Mr. Bennet flinched, and Darcy felt a flash of guilt. Then Mr. Bennet shook his head and with a wry smile said, "Admit it, friend, you are jealous of Mr. Wickham."

Darcy almost growled. He gripped the armrest of the chair tightly. "I assure you that I do not tell you this because of some petty jealousy."

"No, no. I know that. Of course Wickham is a seducer. I half suspected it before you told me a word. I shall give the order to Mrs. Hill that he shall not be admitted. I'll tell my daughters too, much as Lydia and Kitty will squeal."

"I thank you."

Mr. Darcy stood, but before he could head to the door Mr. Bennet added, "Please consider that you are in fact driven by a passion for Elizabeth in this current anger towards Wickham — I do not believe that she has any strong feelings towards Wickham, and if you *talk* with her about it — she expects to be talked to, not dictated to. Civil concourse..."

"I assure you that I have ample prior cause for anger against Wickham."

"No, no. I know." Mr. Bennet stood up and hurried to the door. He briefly touched Mr. Darcy on the arm. "I beg you still, just talk to my daughter. Tell her what you feel. Don't demand her to obey you without reason. If you respect her as a companion... I beg you. I love my daughter, do not hurt her."

"She is to be my wife." Darcy paused. He looked again at Mr. Bennet's worn face. "She is to be my wife. Her happiness and wellbeing will be in my care. Whatever my annoyance at the circumstance, I *will*, I swear to you, care for her as she deserves."

Then he had to face Elizabeth.

They stood alone together in the drawing room, since Mrs. Bennet was still eager to give them the chance to chaperone themselves. The wallpapered walls were stuffed to the corners with decorative wardrobes showing off vulgar decorative figurines and faux expensive plates. The Bennets did have a fine decorative rug, though.

Darcy breathed through his nose. His first instinct was still to demand and dictate. To tell Elizabeth that she would obey him. That was what marriage involved: the woman agreed to submit to and obey her husband, and in turn he cared for her, and he loved her, and he worshipped her body, and he ensured the honorable position in society of their children.

Elizabeth had conspired to marry him; she *deserved* to be dictated to.

If he permitted himself to think in that way, he would fail in the promise he made minutes before to Mr. Bennet. Elizabeth was not a woman who would be happy in being dictated to. He could not protect her happiness and demand her unthinking obedience at the same time.

And, Darcy realized, he would not want to marry a woman who would let him order her around.

"Mr. Wickham has..." Darcy pulled in a deep breath. "I can tell you many stories of his indiscretions. He has wasted large sums of money, and he... he is not a man who you shall have dealings with."

"He has offended me — but you cannot expect me to submit without complaint to your every demand, no matter what it is. If you expect I will, you expect wrongly." Elizabeth's eyes flashed, and she put her hands on her hips, daring him to disagree.

Darcy felt a spasm of indignation, destroying for a moment his earlier intentions to speak to her calmly and as an equal. "I am to be your husband. You ought to trust me. Though I understand that a woman who would entrap an honorable man into marriage is not likely to be a woman who trusts easily."

"You! Why you... *you* are hardly a gentleman. You seem oft to forget, in your insistence that I *trapped* you, that *you* kissed me. How am I to know that you do not kiss every woman you see? How am I to know that you are not as much a rake as Mr. Wickham is." Elizabeth paused. "I mean as you claim Mr. Wickham to be."

"As WIckham *is*."

"Wickham *spoke* to me. He made no high-handed demands." Elizabeth wildly paced back and forth. "You, sir. You, sir! You expect me to simply believe such a calumny against a..." She growled, "Well he at first had every appearance of goodness. And you demand I avoid him with no proof, nothing but your word?"

Darcy took a deep breath. Elizabeth could infuriate him like he had never been infuriated before. Perhaps that was a good thing though. Her red sweet lips, her bright flashing eyes, her white gleaming skin. The temper in both of them made her seem more beautiful to him.

Something changed in Elizabeth's eyes as well as he stared at her, bringing his unwonted temper into submission.

She quirked her lips into a smile. "That passionate gaze will not divert me from winning my point."

"I shall explain *some* of what cause I have against Wickham, and if you insist, I shall have documentary proof sent for from Pemberley as to the details. Letters between us, and the like."

Elizabeth choked out a surprised laugh. "You've kept your correspondence with him?"

"I am not, Madam, in the habit of burning or destroying my letters. And in the case of certain matters of business that passed between us, there were large sums of money changing hands, and I always keep full records of any dealings of that sort."

Now she looked to him, eyes alight in curiosity. "Yes, what happened with your father's will, in your story of the matter. I know you too well now to still believe that you would simply refuse Wickham the parish he claims he was promised without any payment."

"Ah, so that is his accusation. He received three thousand pounds in turn for it, in addition to a further thousand left in the will for his use. I can send for the documents and receipts, and our correspondence settling this business.."

"See!" Elizabeth stamped her foot. She looked almost as annoyed by him explaining himself as she had been when he refused to. "And why would you not simply tell me this all *before*."

"I do not divulge the details of my house's doings to those who have not proven trustworthiness. Further it is not my place to respond to the accusations of such a man."

"*Not* that again." Elizabeth angrily threw her hands in the air. "Arrogant, stiff, *unhelpful*."

Darcy smiled at her.

He could not help it. Not when she became so exasperated, and the red in her cheeks and the sparkles in her eyes lit up. Also he realized that Wickham *had* already done the job of alienating Elizabeth's affections. "Beyond the will. What did Wickham accuse *me* of in detail, I will respond to specific accusations. He never had a serious interest in you, but then you have no, I believe, authentic interest in him, either. He is determined to only marry an heiress."

"So convinced he is just a fortune hunter. What, did he try to court your sister?"

Darcy's face went completely stiff and cold.

So Wickham had been telling the story. He had sworn not to.

Elizabeth's had covered her mouth, and she went pale. "He *did*."

"Madam," Darcy said angrily, "I shall expect you, as a woman of honor, to spread no such suggestions around. They are entirely untrue and—"

"What happened? — twas just a guess. He said nothing on the matter, except he thought her proud and unfriendly."

"It is not my business to tell you."

"Was there real affection between them? Did you separate them simply because you disliked Wickham's lack of prospects?"

"*He* suborned her companion. Mrs. Younge. The woman I paid to be the governor of her morals, she was seduced to be Wickham's *lover*, and then Mr. Wickham, using the unlimited opportunities for access to a shy and impressionable girl of barely fifteen that this immoral woman delivered to him, convinced her, convinced my sister to imagine herself in love with him. I learned only of this scheme when, by luckiest happenstance, I joined her on her holiday in Ramsgate two days before the planned elopement was to happen. She was too good to hide her affections from her brother, now that I was present."

Elizabeth was pale.

"This is what your *harmless, innocent, and kind* friend does. That is what he did. She has yet to recover her confidence in herself, or her old sense of happiness. *That* I blame Wickham for. And now I see him inveigling his way into your ears. And now you have been warned, and you are no girl of fifteen to be so easily fooled. So by God, if you expect me to go through with this, to fulfill your mother's grandest fantasies, and for this stratagem of binding me by lust and requirement of honor into marriage with you, against my judgement, against my character, and against my interests — then by Jove, you will obey me in this and have no more concourse with Mr. Wickham."

Darcy's heart raced. He trembled with rage or jealousy. He could not know which. He was shocked at himself. He had never let his anger at Wickham out in this way. Not even when Colonel Fitzwilliam ranted on about how much he wished he could have caught Wickham and challenged him to a duel — with swords so he would be able to definitely kill the bastard.

Even then his anger against Wickham had not burst forth into voice.

And now jealousy and Elizabeth had brought it out.

She placed a soft hand over his hand.

Instead of crackling with mischief and spirit as they usually did, her eyes were luminous with empathy and understanding. "I swear," she said seriously, "I swear I shall never speak to Mr. Wickham again — even before you told me — I somehow knew this morn that he was not telling the entire truth. I merely was angered by your high-handedness. Wickham has given you ample cause to despise him. And I will stand with you and despise him as well."

Darcy compulsively swallowed, unable to look away from her sweet eyes.

She could not look away from his eyes either.

That hypnotic passion that pulled them together was there. Her lips were soft and red. Her cheeks pale and white, and covered with tears. And her eyes sparkled with something Fitzwilliam Darcy felt deep in his stomach, and that look in her eyes somehow meant the world, though he could not yet *say* precisely how her eyes made everything to change.

He felt vulnerable, as if with her words Elizabeth could hurt him terribly. But she wouldn't. He also knew she wouldn't.

He held his hand out to her face and touched it against her cheek. She nestled her face against his broad hand, and the beauty of her expression made his heart stutter wildly.

Despite everything, all was right with the world and all was at peace.

There was a word, Darcy knew, for what he felt towards Elizabeth. But his mind refused to yet produce that word, to say it either to himself or to her.

Chapter Six

After the revelation about Wickham and Mr. Darcy's sister, Elizabeth begged Darcy to stay for dinner with them, and he accepted despite her mother's squawks at having to prepare a meal fit for an income of ten thousand a year with a warning of merely forty-five minutes.

She did not want him to go.

They were to marry, and there was something between them, and she wanted to explore what it was.

At dinner conversation was awkward, as they sat next to each other.

Elizabeth could not stop thinking about her left hand, hidden under the table cloth. Darcy's knee. Inches away from it.

Elizabeth for a while lost any ability to pay attention to Papa's efforts to prod Darcy into conversation, or her mother's questions about the London season and Mr. Darcy's plans for ensuring Mrs. Darcy was well cared for, and who were his rich friends who she might be able to push the girls onto — Elizabeth stopped Mama at this point.

She could see that Mr. Darcy did not like to hear these suggestions; it made her to appear even more grossly mercenary than Darcy already believed her to be, and it annoyed her too.

Elizabeth redirected Mama towards a description of her plans for the Christmas holiday, and her plans for the happy event which they had decided would occur right before Christmas, since they were to say the first round of the banns on Sunday. Both Elizabeth and Darcy insisted they were to marry by regular church course, even though Mrs. Bennet insisted it would be delightfully more romantic and prestigious to have it done by special license.

Romantic? Maybe.

But a little less respectable, at least by the habits and way of looking at matters of a rural society in Hertfordshire, whatever they may think about special licenses in the *ton*. When two young persons are caught kissing in the library during a ball, if they wish to maintain their sober reputation, they will seek to use the most respectable route possible to achieving the marriage.

Darcy remained quiet the entire time of the dinner, saying few things. His voice was not required by Elizabeth's mother, since even when Mrs. Bennet asked him a question, she instantly launched onto the next topic of conversation, and thus to even answer the woman's queries would have required that he speak over her, but from Darcy's small smiles directed towards her — she was *now* quite assured that those twists of his lips were smiles — she believed him to not in fact be unhappy.

And sometimes, at first by accident, and then quite by purpose, on both their parts, their knees bumped into each other.

It was, in the end, quite the most stressing and thrilling dinner she had ever eaten at Longbourn.

At long, long, long last the dinner ended. It was still late afternoon, so before Elizabeth was forced to leave Darcy to the tender mercies of her father — who had spent the entire dinner with an annoyed frown towards Mr. Darcy — Papa had insisted on thinking ill of Darcy for the entire matter, as if she had not been just as reckless in kissing him while alone in a room as he had been in kissing *her* while alone in a room.

The whole blame went to Bingley, for leasing the place, and then not tossing the bear rug into storage.

But Bingley was too nice, and too likely to marry Jane for Elizabeth to remain angry at him. And anyways it really was the housekeeper's fault, and before that the blame really belonged to whoever turned the bear into a rug — but she had no idea who it was, probably the sad old baronet who'd died a few years before with no sons to leave with the pile or the title he'd gained from his father.

And *he* had been too sad to blame for his atrocious taste in library floor coverings.

In the end, there was no one left to blame but the *rug*.

And it was impossible to remain properly enraged at a piece of furniture for a great duration of time. So really, Papa should simply accept that Darcy could be sometimes sweet, if he also was frequently ungentlemanly, overbearing, and quite... masculine.

So maybe she could *not* expect Papa to begin to see Darcy in a positive light for the same reasons that Elizabeth had begun to consider him kindly.

Still Papa should not look at Darcy like he was dragging her to perdition. The two of them would get on quite well together... in between their ferocious arguments... arguments she actually, almost liked.

Matters could be much worse, and she wanted to talk to Darcy, on her own again, and thank him for telling her about Miss Darcy's past — even though he had not meant to. And for bravely scaring off the sneering snakelike seducer, Mr. George Wickham, from near her vulnerable, female person, which Mr. Darcy most certainly *had* meant to do.

She needed to get him in private, away from Mama, who talked far too much. And away from Lydia also. Who talked far too much too, and who was still convinced that Darcy was a terrible person for what he did to poor Wicky. Especially since *now* Wicky wouldn't be allowed to visit them at the house ever again.

"Mama! I believe Darcy and I shall take a walk," Elizabeth exclaimed the instant he and Mr. Bennet, unspeaking and unsmiling entered the room together after twenty minutes of sitting together. "The weather is quite too fine to stay inside the entire day."

Everyone looked at her. Mr. Darcy raised one eyebrow again in that skeptical manner of his.

The gusting wind rattled the windows. Once more.

The sky was grey. Not a thunderstorm probably, but they'd be facing cold sleet in another hour or so, and Darcy should return to Netherfield immediately if he wanted to escape the rain. But he had come armed with a fine well-oiled long furred coat, and that combined with Darcy's robustness meant that Elizabeth was quite sure *he* would never face a cold from horseback riding in this weather, not like Jane had.

Elizabeth realized she was unconsciously licking her lips again. In front of her whole family.

With a blush Elizabeth looked down.

Darcy said in a calm voice, "I entirely agree that the weather today is far too fine to not enjoy the outdoors. Perhaps a short stroll in the shrubberies, which keeps us *near* the house, just in case we wish to escape from the *sun*, would be a fine idea."

"Then I can chaperone you from my study window," Mr. Bennet said sharply. "Don't wander out of view."

Elizabeth and Darcy went to the doors and armed themselves against the moderate cold.

As they stepped out into the gusting wind, Darcy grinned at her and said, "The weather is too nice to miss?"

"You are the one who was worried about needing to escape from the sun."

The two looked at each other and laughed merrily.

Elizabeth was not sure if she'd ever seen Darcy laugh before, but it made him very handsome when he did.

"Mama had been talking too much about clothes for me to think up a better excuse." Elizabeth grimaced and, looking wide eyed and trustingly into Darcy's eyes, asked, "Would you mind, that is mind terribly, if I only wore sackcloth and ashes for the first six months following our wedding, just to spite her?"

He did not reply. She looked down and then up at him again. There was the skeptically raised one eyebrow again. "Yes," Mr. Darcy said at last, firmly. "I would mind terribly."

"Oh, well," Elizabeth said, sadly giving up one of her great recent dreams.

"I had been," Darcy added after they had made the forty foot circuit around the shrubberies in front of Mr. Bennet's watching window twice more, "expecting you to be eager for the opportunity to dress to the standards that the world expects to see in a Mrs. Darcy. Women and clothes, and all."

"Heavens! You sound as fashion obsessed as my mother. I shall *not* spend the next six weeks spending your money while accumulating a dress for every day of the month."

"I quite agree," Darcy said, taking her arm, and keeping her pulled close to him, providing a small guard against the gusting winds that bit through her coat. "Only having a dress for almost every day of the month would be quite sufficient. You will not shame yourself if you repeat as many as three times in the course of a moon."

Helplessly Elizabeth giggled.

Darcy had a very satisfied look on his face.

"I am sorry the conversation at the meal was not more... or maybe, less..."

"I truly must thank you for inviting me and making me to stay." Darcy smiled at her, openly showing his pearly white teeth. Just as fine and well cared for as Wickham's. And the rest of him was completely superior. "Whatever your mother's deficits as a conversant, at present she is preferred to *Miss Bingley*."

Darcy pursed his lips, as though he had said something he should not.

Elizabeth cattily smiled, "Tell me more?"

"I should not speak ill of my hostess, and I should not have said so much."

"Come now. A secret: I do not believe she likes me very much. And, I tell you in confidence, I do not like *her* greatly in return. I now begin to suspect she was *jealous* of all the attention you paid to me."

Darcy laughed. He actually laughed!

His laugh was a full resonant sound, which was much louder than the gusts of wind rustling the almost bare boughs of winter, and louder than the grinding of the gravelled pathway beneath their boots.

His laugh warmed her more than the chill wind chapped and cooled her cheeks.

"I believe you are quite right," Darcy said laughingly. "She expected this before I did — she was warning me that if I was not cautious I would marry you. And I said the mind of a lady is rapid."

"It jumps from admiration to love to matrimony?"

"In a word."

"She was assiduous in courting *your* admiration. 'Oh, you write so finely. I adore your sister so much. Such neat lines. I could never write so much' — by the by, if you were hoping for an illiterate wife who will be incapable of bothering you with long missives while you are away on business, I am afraid I shall suit you poorly."

"Those long missives that I shall expect every time we are apart and you as well, you both shall suit me very well."

Both blushed.

They walked their way in another circuit around the smallish lawn. All of the time they both were aware of Mr. Bennet's eyes, no doubt watching them from the study, though the sun falling on his window created a reflection that made it impossible to look in on him through the window to tell if he was engrossed in his reading, or in watching his daughter and her suitor.

"Miss Bingley is quite upset with me," Darcy said at last, "though today the meal would be properly cooked, since Mr. Hurst said he planned to stir himself from couch and cards to oversee Cook in ensuring that he definitely gets a good meal today, after yesterday."

"And *what* occurred yesterday? How did Miss Bingley vent her spleen?"

"The worst possible fate to the man who had scorned her was for him to eat the leftovers of the previous night. *Cold.*"

Elizabeth dramatically shivered. "That is terrible. All greasy, and ugh. I always make them heat up my cold cuts properly."

"Really? I find cold beef the day after delightful. Especially in winter when it stays properly preserved, and gets quite cold. There is a different flavor and the seasonings taste more intense, and — you do not agree."

Elizabeth flinched back in disgust from his description. "I shall not be serving cold leftovers to our guests during the winter months."

She blushed. *Our guests.* Darcy blushed as well, and they glanced at each other and then looked at the ground and everywhere else but each other.

But then Darcy smiled and patted her hand, the touch of his gloved fingers made her stomach jump.

They continued along the walk, looking side to side, and quietly enjoying the cold day.

A gust of wind flapped her cloak against his jacket, and Elizabeth liked, for a strange reason, their clothes being entangled.

After silence took them two more times around the lawn, Darcy said, "I have written of our marriage to all of my aunts, uncles and cousins. Especially to my uncle's youngest son, Colonel Richard Fitzwilliam, I hope he shall have opportunity to take leave from his regiment for our wedding — he should, they are at present stationed to guard London — so that you can meet him, he is my dearest confidant and friend, along with Bingley. My sister. I have not written to her yet about the marriage."

"Because..." Elizabeth squared her shoulders. Best to take the matter by the horns and say it openly instead of pretending. Theirs was not a normal marriage, and if Elizabeth was deeply unsure whether she wanted or not to marry Mr. Darcy, he must equally feel uncertain. "You are unhappy, and you do not want to tell her."

"No."

"You are not unhappy then?" Elizabeth smiled at him.

"I am unsure — but there are matters besides the question of 'happiness'."

Not an impassioned lover's declaration, but the statement of a reasonable man. Elizabeth said so, teasingly.

"Yes," Darcy replied with his quirked smile. "You mean an unreasonably reasonable man? For a reasonably reasonable man would have made a better lover's declaration to his betrothed? But I have no doubt about my plans to marry. We shall marry, and we shall make a companionable couple. In any event, I am not in the habit of requesting advice from my sister on such matters, nor of hesitating to inform those about me of news of significance. So I shall have no hesitation in only emphasizing in my communications with her those aspects of the matter which make me seem entirely happy. She shall not be greatly surprised, as I have been writing in my letters to her about you and how I wish her to emulate your character—"

"You have?" Elizabeth felt it again. That glow in her stomach.

"Yes I have."

He frowned at her. And Elizabeth felt that spasm of anxiety combined with indignation and anger. The words were hidden, but Elizabeth was quite sure that she could hear the thought that was in his mind: *That was before I became convinced you had tricked me into a marriage.*

The damned man had kissed her first. Or at least at the same moment she kissed him.

But this moment of anger flitted away. Darcy smiled at her again and said, "No, Wickham is the source of my problem."

"Oh!" Elizabeth let out a long breath. "Does she still love him much? Do you think she would wish to renew the acquaintanceship if they were reunited?"

He shook his head. A decisive motion. "No. I trust her good sense. And her words." — *But not mine.* — "She has told me she thinks upon him with nothing but regret for her own stupidity, and I shall believe her. She is honest and admits her faults. I know I can trust her on that account."

There was a stumbling pause. Georgiana admitted her honest faults. Elizabeth did not admit her fault. She did not admit that she had trapped him into this marriage. So he couldn't trust her.

Conceited, hubristic, high-handed, etc. Her anger at Darcy had a stale feel. This anger fatigued her. They were to marry, she had no choice but to marry him, and she should simply accept that he would distrust her for his own mistaken understanding, and she ought to focus on the admirable traits he had, and the ways he liked her.

"In any case," Darcy added, "I do not want to face her with Wickham, and I cannot guarantee that she would not see him, perhaps with his arm around another woman, simply to torment her. I want to spare her every pain. But if she was not invited to my wedding, she would misunderstand, and that would give her a different pain."

Elizabeth smiled. "You are a caring brother. Though a little too controlling, you think all matters are a matter for *you* to decide."

"What do you mean?"

"I mean you should plainly speak in your letter about Wickham's presence and your concern, and let her choose whether to risk being faced with such a thing— I am certain she shall wish to come and be here for your marriage. She must be a loving sister with such a brother, but she shall not see Wickham unexpectedly, and this chance to make her own choice in such a matter will encourage her sense of independence and trust in herself — as you trust *her*, you must wish her also to trust herself."

Darcy straightened his chest tall. The anxiety that had been present in his manner, somehow visible to Elizabeth was entirely gone. "Elizabeth," he smilingly said, "you are a treasure. I knew your advice would be worthwhile."

"You did." Elizabeth met his smile tilting her head. "Was it such a difficult decision to ask my opinion?"

"No, I know you to be a loving sister, and one who would happily correct the deficiencies in your own sisters if you were given some control over them. I have seen you — sweaty and glowing with exercise — walk three miles at once to the side of a beloved sister—"

"Now do not give me undue credit!" cried Elizabeth. "Jane is a perfect dear. Any person would travel three times three miles on foot for her sake."

Darcy smiled at her, warmly and approvingly.

They both looked towards the study window from which Mr. Bennet, possibly, looked out.

No chance to kiss.

"In any case," Darcy added after a pause. "You are a clever and sensible woman whose judgement I value enormously. There is no other woman in the world entire who I would ask so quickly for advice upon Georgiana's wellbeing."

There they were again.

The butterflies in her stomach. Except this time the butterflies had been joined by kittens wrestling together. She wanted to gush a bit with happiness, and she knew that was stupid as he still distrusted her — but he'd realize, eventually he would realize that she was always honest to him, and that she would never lie to him, or use a stratagem in such a serious matter as marriage.

Elizabeth realized she was falling in love with her betrothed.

Chapter Seven

Early the next morning on a panting and mud splattered horse, Darcy's robust cousin Colonel Richard Fitzwilliam arrived to Netherfield. Miss Bingley saw through the doorway who the visitor was and hid, while Mr. Hurst laughingly greeted the colonel, who entered the hallway on his energetic restlessly pacing legs, like a wolf.

"Darcy!" Colonel Fitzwilliam gripped Darcy's wrists. "The game is still afoot, and the hunt is yet on. I can unhitch this trap of yours. I've thought all morning upon it on the ride here."

"You can?"

"No cousin of *mine* is going to marry a compromising adventuress. We'll compromise her compromise, and spring you free of the parson's mousetrap. Don't look so down — you won't need to marry her."

"In my letter, you may recall, I said I was not entirely averse to the marriage."

"Nonsense! Fritterdash! You simply think you are trapped by the chit, and want to make yourself feel the best you can about the matter — I mean really, planning to marry a girl who you think is a liar, a cheat, and of low moral character — would such a being be Georgiana's sister? No! The mother of your children? No! And even more importantly, the mother of my cousins once removed? No!" Colonel Fitzwilliam pounded his balled up fist against his palm. "And again I say it: No!"

"How," Darcy asked with dread, scared of the possibility of not needing to marry Elizabeth, "could you allow me to escape from this marriage without an appearance of dishonor?"

"Simple: I know a smuggler in these parts who has a man who… well, let us simply say that this man is likely to turn up dead somewhere sometime this month. We dig a smuggler's cave in the Bennet estate —

I have men, close-lipped men, who would do that quite quiet like, and fast, fast. No problem. Done in two days. Then this man will be thrown dead onto these Bennets' lawn, and when the magistrates investigate, we ensure they find the smuggler stash on the land, and other evidence which points to the Bennets being a family of smugglers. They are thrown into Newgate, and you have an excuse that nobody would blame you for to end the engagement. Simple. Simple."

"*That* is your plan?" When Colonel Fitzwilliam nodded, Darcy replied in a relieved tone, "My name, I am afraid, would yet remain connected with a scandal of the worst sort."

"Eh! Lily livered. Anyone who can't survive a little talking about doesn't deserve to be left in peace."

"I would quite strongly prefer that you do not throw any dead smugglers on Elizabeth's lawn. Though—"

"Nonsense, man!"

Colonel Fitzwilliam's voice roared, silencing Darcy. It was not something he was used to. Since the death of his father only Colonel Fitzwilliam ever spoke over him like that. Though Elizabeth liked to talk over him as well.

"Richard, would you not shout so—"

"Nonsense!" Colonel Fitzwilliam grabbed Darcy's arm and dragged him from the hallway and through the door. "You don't let a compromiser *win*! Nonsense, man! Nonsense. You are my cousin. That exact same Fitzwilliam blood flows in your noble body as flows through my elastic veins! You never let an enemy win. Not if you have to saw off your own hand to escape their trap, like my great uncle did when they tried to force him to marry."

"He died of the blood loss."

"Better that than *defeat*."

God, no. There was one thing Colonel Fitzwilliam could *not* stand, and it was to lose. If he thought his cousin was *losing* in an important matter, every consideration of honor, of prudence, of figuring out what Darcy actually wanted would be thrown aside in a desperate attempt to *win*.

Darcy dug in his heels on the marble of Bingley's portico, and despite his fervent vitality, like a wild tiger prepared to leap upon his prey, Colonel Fitzwilliam could no more pull Darcy than a tiger could move a noble elephant. Or something, that metaphor made matters sound of more significance than they actually were. "This is not a matter of winning or losing. It is a matter of marriage. Of my choice and my future life, and of my honor—"

"She tricked you into needing to offer for you. Her *victory* — you must strike back, and prove that the Darcy name — and the associated Fitzwilliam name, cannot be, and can never be, tread upon."

Colonel Fitzwilliam looked out upon the lands surrounding Netherfield, his eyes travelling like those of a hawk, over glen and dale, field and forest, town and country. The view from their high perch on Netherfield's portico was quite excellent. Colonel Fitzwilliam honestly, Darcy could tell, honestly considered roaring defiance at the skies.

Darcy should have known he'd throw his cousin into this state with his letter, but he'd been so disturbed himself that he had only thought on his need for friendship and advice. "Richard. Richard, calm down. My honor is at question too. I *chose* to kiss her. Her stratagem never could have worked without my own weakness. If it was a defeat, it was a part of my own nature which defeated another part, and I have no desire to prove that the Darcy name can never be tread upon by a Darcy, because that would be a ridiculous expectation."

For a moment Colonel Fitzwilliam continued to wildly clench and unclench his fingers, like a tiger pushing his claws in and out. Darcy feared this was going to be like when Colonel Fitzwilliam spent two weeks hunting Wickham through London after Georgiana's near elopement.

Aha!

He *could* defeat Fitzwilliam's mood, and thus win. Divert, that is, and thus allow them both to win... give Fitzwilliam something he wanted in exchange for calming down. Feed the tiger a chunk of tasty meat to allow the antelope to escape.

Mention that Wickham was here, and *that* would distract the wild animal.

Colonel Fitzwilliam relaxed before Darcy mentioned Wickham's presence in the neighborhood. "All right. I'll see her for myself and decide. But you are being absurd to marry a woman you do not trust — that is no sound basis for a sound marriage."

He bound forward, lithely down the portico, hopping down the stairs three at a time, somehow without seeming to have any risk of stumbling, and then marching off to the stables to collect his sweaty horse once more. Darcy followed at a quick pace which allowed him to use each downstairs step. He'd go up the stairs two at a time, but going down like that was simply begging for a fall that would bash the brains out. At least if you were a normal man.

His cousin was not a normal man.

*****

Elizabeth and Jane were walking together back from another shopping trip. Since her previous one had been disrupted by Darcy's impressively and masculinely intense send off of George Wickham, Elizabeth still needed to engage in book purchasing to comfort her soul.

Hopefully the foul candied man would permanently avoid her — the more Elizabeth thought about it, the angrier she became at Wickham.

She saw Lydia's face, a girl barely out in society, so very young, so very unschooled, and simply guessing at what matters the future would hold. Someone convincing such a naïve girl that they were in love, and that they should elope.

A man like that, a calculating man, seeking to destroy a woman's life, nor for love, nor for affection but for greed simply.

George Wickham: Candied manure. The first taste was sweet. The second vomitous.

Fortunately this day Elizabeth had been able to successfully reach Mr. Hyde's bookshop. After browsing for a quarter of an hour, she bought two novels written by entertaining authors of dramatic romances whose names Elizabeth was quite sure would not survive the test of time, a volume of recent poetry by Byron, and a large expensive text complete with many plates on the great works of art of the Dutch masters of the Republican period before William of Orange established himself as a king.

Elizabeth's fingers already itched to page through the paintings while sitting comfortably next to the fire in Papa's study. She had spent perhaps more than she should, and would not be able to festoon herself with ribbons or a new bonnet without borrowing from someone for the next weeks. After that, she would have plenty of money for all the silks she wanted, even if Mr. Darcy's cruelty extended so far as he had suggested it would to *only* settling a six or seven *hundred* pounds on her as pin money.

The horror, how would she survive upon so *little*? How would she manage to spend so much seemed at the moment a deeper difficulty.

Hopefully Darcy would call today again. *He* enjoyed their passionate labial (lip to lip, in the vernacular) interludes at least half as much as

Elizabeth did.

And there was Darcy's famed Pemberley library, which he could hardly expect to restrict her from, and that would be the second great consolation she could expect from the marriage, after the low passionate interludes with which she had tempted him into this marriage relationship. That library would likely, Elizabeth estimated, keep her from requiring the purchase of new books for at least a twelve month following her marriage.

But the new library was in Derbyshire, not present in Hertfordshire. So her money went to book purchases *now* on this blustery day that billowed their cloaks about them, and tossed their dresses up to expose their silk stockinged ankles.

Elizabeth enthusiastically discoursed to Jane while they walked homewards upon the soothing properties of new books. From behind them the clacking of hoofbeats approaching sounded. Such was not an unusual occurrence, Elizabeth continued speaking as Jane glanced backwards, perhaps hoping Bingley had at last returned after his trip to London that had taken up the past three — *three* — whole days.

Jane's eyes widened as a deep rumbling voice boomed out from behind Elizabeth, "Jove! Darcy, are you crazy? She is the most beautiful woman my eyes have ever set touch upon, and that by a great margin. That she needed to ensnare you by trick into marriage is a great condemnation of your denseness."

Elizabeth turned around to see Darcy and a gentleman in the fine redcoat and splendid plumed cap of a senior officer in the regulars dismounting from their horses. Darcy replied in an annoyed manner to his companion. "Not *her!* That is her sister. She is the other one." A pause as Darcy glared at the man. He continued in a low voice which Elizabeth thought was not intended to carry to the women waiting the approach of the two gentlemen. "And Elizabeth is prettier than Jane. I have no notion why the general attitude prefers Miss Bennet, but it is utterly wrongheaded."

"Ha." The officer's voice boomed out. "I begin to suspect you are truly in love, for only the blindness of such strong preference could lead you to prefer Miss Elizabeth to the other."

As the two walked up to them Darcy added in a truly irritated voice, "Miss Bennet smiles too much."

"Smiles too much? By Jove! What is wrong with you?"

As a result of these overhearings rather to purpose, both Elizabeth and Jane had the heightened color of a blush when the gentlemen bowed to them smilingly. Elizabeth could not help but be pleased by Darcy's *present* strong partiality for her, despite the disparagement of Jane, which she usually could never stand. And Jane surely had enough balm for her vanity in the striking preference of Mr. Darcy's striking companion.

Jane was in fact rosily smiling, yet keeping the blond serenity that was her habit.

The officer was a man of short to middling height, whose face was square and robust, instead of striking and noble like Darcy's, or finely boned and smooth like Mr. Wickham's. He had a large bald spot visible on the back of his head once he swept his cap off in greeting. His shoulders were almost as broad as those of a professional pugilist, and there was a grace and smoothness in his stride and movements that made Elizabeth feel as though he were a man who could be dangerous in sudden movements. His eyes and voice were intense.

Without giving Darcy an opportunity to speak or make the introduction, the officer swept a bow to Jane and said, "My cousin is laggard in giving introduction, so I must make myself known to you — the impropriety I confess, but I am a simple officer, a soldier, who has faced death, eye to eye, as if I were wrestling with a wolf lunging for my throat, day after day, battle after battle for years. Such moments give clarity. The forms of society have no importance next to making the most of one's life moment to moment, thus I presume to approach any woman who I wish to know nearer. My name is Colonel Richard Fitzwilliam of his Majesty's 25th Foot, I am the third son of the Earl of Matlock, and the cousin of this tall taciturn man next to me, who I am told is to be your brother."

Jane blushed and smiled at this remarkable introduction. She replied, "I am Miss Jane Bennet of Longbourn. As we are to be *almost* related, I suppose I may reply to you without a proper introduction — but oh, I am so sorry that you must face such dangers. I wish wars were not fought, and men such as you were not placed in danger constantly."

"I wish that as well. I wish I might stay within our dear England year upon year, and throw myself upon the feet of such pretty women as yourself, for your face is the most stunning ever seen since that face which launched a thousand ships upon deadly war. But alas, if Englishmen shall never be slaves, then Englishmen must fight the little ogre across the channel. And to me falls that task."

There was another blushing smile from Jane, but she said nothing further. Elizabeth could tell that her sister was not quite sure how to respond to this hyperbolic praise, even though she was used to a great deal of admiration from men.

Darcy said to Jane, "Don't take him so seriously." Then to his cousin, "And she is to be my sister. Treat Miss Bennet with respect."

"I shall treat the silken skinned Jane Bennet with great respect."

Darcy frowned at him. The Colonel Fitzwilliam shrugged and smiled back. Then he turned his intense and slightly wild eyes upon Elizabeth. "But to business. I wish to speak to you, Miss Elizabeth, as we walk. For I have heard information from Mr. Darcy that suggests your character is not of the type which I would wish for in a relation."

Elizabeth growled at Darcy. "Must you defame me to your relations?"

Darcy replied evenly, "I have only spoken the truth while seeking advice. Nothing beyond a bare recounting of the true facts."

"But," Colonel Fitzwilliam said, "Darcy said nothing of your beauty, which while it is eclipsed by the Helenic features and figure of your sister, is nonetheless of remark worthy rarity. And we both know, you and I, that he is not — ah, how should I put this without damaging my cousin's fragile sense of self-worth?"

"*Richard,*" Darcy's voice echoed warningly.

"He would make a poor rake," Colonel Fitzwilliam said at last, winking at Elizabeth, who could not help but giggle. "I would neither use him to gather in leaves to their burning, nor to gather in innocent women to their *burning.*"

"Richard!"

"See?" Colonel Fitzwilliam gestured towards Darcy. "A proper rake would not blush at such an obliquely improper joke."

He took Elizabeth's arm, and they walked up the path together. "But tell me truly — and know, I can smell dishonesty in a woman just like I can smell a trap from the French — did you seek to entrap my cousin into marriage?"

"No!" Elizabeth sharply pulled her arm from his. "I have no choice but to go through this engagement. I *understand* that matters appear such that my credit in the neighborhood would be entirely ruined after several respectable persons saw *Darcy* kissing me — but if I could, this man, who chooses to defame me to his own relations, would be the last man I would marry."

Elizabeth saw from the corner of her eye Darcy wince.

Good.

Darcy said apologetically, "I truly did not mean to defame you — I promise, none of my other relations know anything of the irregularity in our engagement."

Colonel Fitzwilliam said, "You speak decidedly for one marrying someone so rich. How *did* you end up kissing my cousin?"

Jane blushed at this line of questioning. And Elizabeth felt extremely awkward talking about this at all, especially in front of her sister. "A gentleman," she replied to the officer, "should not ask such questions."

"But a gentleman, who is entirely committed to the wellbeing of his cousin — a cousin who we both understand to be incapable of dealing with the darker wiles of a clever female—"

"*Richard.*"

"You are the one who insists you were tricked into kissing her. It would not take a trick to make me—"

"*Richard!*" Darcy looked authentically offended at the suggestion of Colonel Fitzwilliam kissing her.

Elizabeth rolled her eyes and replied. "As though my mother could keep a count up to five minutes. Or me. It is the most ridiculous idea in the world that I timed my tripping over that grotesque bear's rug for when she planned to enter."

"Ah!" Colonel Fitzwilliam nodded. "As a military man I grip precisely onto your meaning. To create a plan which requires the close timing and coordination of two separated parties, that is a difficult matter. But still, with your family connection, you could have practiced keeping the time clock together, and a pair committed to entrapping rich gentlemen would have ample incentive to develop the skill."

Elizabeth replied with an annoyed huff. "If you insist, I am sure it is *possible*. But I would say it is not likely…"

Colonel Fitzwilliam held his strong fingered hands out wide, showing that he both agreed and did not. He had thick well-muscled wrists.

"In *any* case. Even if I am the deceptive wily female Darcy claims, *he* is the dishonorable man who kisses women without any intention of offering them marriage. If I can overcome my reasonable objections to marriage to such a man, then he ought to overcome his own hypocritical objections."

"That," Colonel Fitzwilliam said as they turned onto the road that ran along Longbourn's thick shrubbery, "is an excellent point. What do you have to say to that, cousin?"

Darcy ground his jaws together.

"Well?"

"I have fully admitted that my honor was compromised, and *that* and not the scandal or threat of scandal is the reason I choose to marry Miss Elizabeth."

"As for me," Elizabeth sharply replied, without being particularly honest, "I would not marry him if *I* had any choice."

Colonel Fitzwilliam took her arm and made her to stop walking. He stared into her eyes intently with his deep blue eyes searching her. Without letting his gaze waver, he said quietly, "Is that truly your feelings?"

Elizabeth stared back into his eyes, but what she saw in her mind was Darcy's eyes as he bent his lips to hers in the candlelight in the Netherfield library. She felt his touch. His strong arms, his clever mind, his tall person, the kindness that she was realizing he had towards many, and the fundamental sense of honor that he held, which likely was why he was so bothered by her insisting that she had not trapped him when he thought she had.

Her eyes dropped to the ground and she shook her head. "No, no. That is not the only reason I marry him."

"Then be honest to your own feelings. At least to yourself. You both ought not engage in such self-deception."

Colonel Fitzwilliam let go of her arm, and took Jane's. "I now understand matters between your sister and my cousin, and they are quite designed one for the other. So from business to pleasure, let me discourse with *you*."

As they walked the remaining yards to Longbourn, Jane said quickly, "Oh, do you really think they are? I am so worried. Worried for both of them — I want everyone to be happy, especially someone so good as Lizzy, and—"

"They will be happy together, though I suspect the course of true love shall not run smooth. But in the end they will be entirely happy."

"Oh, I am glad."

Upon their entry Mrs. Bennet and her other daughters were introduced to Colonel Fitzwilliam. After Mrs. Bennet had enquired of him, and understood that Colonel Fitzwilliam was both unmarried and with weaker prospects than Mr. Bingley she grew concerned at the exaggerated manner in which Colonel Fitzwilliam made what was probably a pretence of courtship towards Jane. "Enough, enough of this, talk to my Lydia. Jane, you must go elsewhere. Lydia, this is a *colonel*. You would very much like to sit next to Colonel Fitzwilliam and talk to him."

"I do not care," Lydia replied to Mrs. Bennet, "though he *is* an officer. For he does not fill his red coat nearly as finely as Mr. Wickham does. His shoulders are too wide and muscular. Wickham's features are much softer and sweeter — I am entirely committed to dancing with him at the *next* assembly, which he will certainly come to, as Mr. Darcy and Lizzy will already be gone to that big pile you wander on and on about."

"Lydia," Mrs. Bennet said, "you cannot ignore a man of ten times Wickham's consequence, for a penniless man, no matter how—"

Elizabeth had noted as her mother droned on the effect that Lydia's speech had on Colonel Fitzwilliam. He seemed to gain two inches in height, and the look that passed across his face was that of a cat spotting a mouse far from its hole: The purest and happiest delight.

His hands he clenched and unclenched, like claws.

"Mr. Wickham. Mr. Wickham is in the militia regiment quartered here?"

"La! You know him! Of course you do," Lydia said, "since Mr. Darcy was so cruel to him, and you are—"

"Mr. *George* Wickham?"

Lydia seemed rather put out by this sharp question. "Yes, I already said—"

"Tell now. Tell. Mr. George Wickham. So high" — the colonel put his hand a few inches above the top of his head — "a fine manner, girlishly attractive face, straight nose, peachy skin, like that of an easily bruised fruit, fine dark hair, roughly the color of fresh manure before it has had opportunity to dry out? He is fastidious about his clothing and hair?"

"La! He looks much nicer than *you*."

"But that is his appearance?"

"And his manners are much better, an —"

"Aha! At last!" His eyes came up, full of an unholy, happy light. He pulled his lips back in a vicious snarl. "George Wickham is in this neighborhood!"

Elizabeth and Lydia eyed his glee, worriedly.

"I like you, Miss Elizabeth. Approve of you and my cousin, even if he is a nitwit about... all matters of interest to the gentler, smarter sex, he isn't a bad sort. Welcome to our family. I now shall consider you as a Fitzwilliam in honor! And you are a diamond also. A diamond. But off! I must off, to find my prey before he hears I am here."

Shrugging Darcy followed his cousin out.

"Deuced fool you are," Colonel Fitzwilliam said, vaulting onto his horse with a one handed leap onto the back. "She didn't trap you into anything. Innocent as a lamb of everything but eyes for your person — Hiiiyaaaa."

And with that shout he galloped out of the barn and down the road to Meryton.

Darcy shouted at Colonel Fitzwilliam's back, "You are just taken in by a pretty face!"

It proved to not be difficult for Colonel Fitzwilliam to find Wickham.

Mr. Wickham was, unsuspecting of the horror that was about to descend upon him, strolling down the road, chest out, smilingly winking at girls passing on the street, with four other officers, who all looked up towards him as though he were their leader.

Darcy almost, though not quite, felt sorry for him.

"George! Wickham!" The shout rang along the street.

Like a rabbit who sees the hawk descending upon him, Wickham froze.

"You owe me a debt of honor!" Colonel Fitzwilliam roared at Wickham. He bound forward and seized in an instant Wickham by his neck, and held him a foot up from the ground as easily as a ragdoll. "You know what you did! I will kill you twice over though if you defame the name of the woman by describing this matter to your fellows. Three times! Three times dead. Swords. Tomorrow. In the morning meet me, or admit to all the world, *all* the world, that you are a slimy sewer rat! A rat whose cowardice is *endless*! Tomorrow!"

The windows rattled at the shout.

Darcy had never seen a face — not even on a dead man — so white as Wickham's. His eyes brought Hamlet to mind: *Make thy two eyes, like stars, start from their spheres.*

The soldiers who were Wickham's friends looked between them, staring at the colonel with faces that mixed indignation at seeing one of their fellows handled so roughly by a stranger with awed admiration at how well the stranger roughly handled him. Colonel Fitzwilliam hurled Wickham to the ground, almost as an afterthought, but hard enough that he skidded on his fine pants for three yards, before leaping to his feet and scurrying in the other direction at a fast run.

Darcy smiled.

He had already scared Wickham once in this week, but though Darcy liked to think highly of himself, he knew that he simply didn't have it in him to be quite as terrifyingly intimidating as Colonel Fitzwilliam.

As Wickham ran off, Colonel Fitzwilliam pointed at one of them. "You, flat nosed soldier."

"Denny, sir. Lieutenant Denny."

"You are his second, make sure he is there for me to skewer tomorrow morning, or make sure he leaves the ranks. He is no worthy man to fight or die next to. And he doesn't pay his gambling debts — ever."

At this all four of the men blanched, looked at each other, and looked at Wickham's retreating form with growls.

They followed him.

"See." Colonel Fitzwilliam smirked. "There shall now be no further problem for us with Wickham."

Darcy pursed his lips and shrugged. "Richard, he *is* my father's godson. I would prefer you did not actually kill him tomorrow, and I think—"

"What? Of course not. That would hardly be a kind wedding present. A dead man? No. You may think I am almost barbaric, but Mother raised me better than *that*. He'll run till he finds a sewer to hide in in London tomorrow. He *is* a sewer rat whose cowardice is endless."

Darcy looked at Wickham again. He had known all along that asking Colonel Fitzwilliam for advice and help would make everything seem better, and it had. "Thank you. This is a *fine* wedding present."

As Colonel Fitzwilliam promised, Wickham disappeared the next morning. He had not disappeared quite fast enough. According to a rumor that no one could prove, but which also no one doubted, he had been caught and beaten severely by his comrades who had summed it up together and found that he had already managed to accumulate more than two hundred pounds in gambling debts to them in the short time he had been part of their company.

A compulsive gambler, but *not* a good one at judging odds.

Denny and Captain Carter smirkingly talked about how he was gone, and how they had restored the honor of the company by properly sending "Rattail" off, as he now required a proper nickname. One that referenced Colonel Fitzwilliam's impressive assault on Wickham.

Chapter Eight

The day following Colonel Fitzwilliam's arrival and Wickham's departure, Bingley at last returned from his business in London. He was delighted to find Colonel Fitzwilliam present, as he had always liked the officer very much when the two of them had come in contact with each other through Darcy.

"Fitzwilliam, deuced glad to see you!" Mr. Bingley exclaimed happily. "Deuced glad. Darcy called you in with his note about marrying Miss Elizabeth? Fine girl, isn't she? And quite like Darcy in mind."

"Quite like. I am convinced they will suit very well."

The party adjourned from the entrance hall to the drawing room, and Bingley greeted his sour faced sisters, and his florid faced brother-in-law.

Bingley asked Colonel Fitzwilliam, "Did you also meet the oldest Bennet daughter?"

"The prettiest woman — the very prettiest who I have ever seen. The clear eyed and ever smiling Jane Bennet."

Mr. Bingley was not entirely satisfied by Colonel Fitzwilliam's praise, as it was rather too warm, coming from a fellow man who Bingley, let us confess it, considered himself slightly inferior to, for the taste of a lover. "Yes well," Bingley coughed. "I have decided to marry Miss Bennet."

"Oh no!" Miss Bingley explained, "You cannot!"

Bingley shook his head annoyedly. "I had believed you to like her very much. You always have declared yourself willing to know her better."

"I have nothing against dear Jane, but her connections..." Miss Bingley shuddered. "You must give over this whole intention. I tell you, you should go back to London."

"And then what? She'll be there at her sister's wedding. And I will be there for Darcy. Nonsense, Caro. I'm marrying Jane."

"Good for you," Colonel Fitzwilliam said enthusiastically. "The delicate featured and fine figured Miss Bennet deserves a kind and capable gentleman for husband. Does she like you?"

"I believe she does." Bingley grinned.

Darcy felt the need to speak, to crush Bingley's hopes. But before he could Miss Bingley cried out angrily, "How could you make such a decision, and without asking *me*!"

"Asking you?"

"As your nearest relation, as the one who will be most affected by your marriage, and—"

"Really, you make too much a production of this. I'd already decided, but, Darcy, I am so glad you are to marry Miss Elizabeth. We shall be brothers, Darcy. Think on that: Brothers!"

"Yes, but—"

"Look at it!" Bingley pulled a jeweler's case from his coat and proudly displayed a purple velvet box containing a ring. "I wanted this made before I returned, which obliged me stay a day extra in London."

It was a gold ring edged with precious stones and a lock of Bingley's reddish brown hair was contained within the ring behind a piece of glass.

"It's a hair ring, I shall give it to my Jane, soon as she accepts me, for I presume to *hope* upon her acceptance, and she shall wear it on the finger closest to her heart for me, and a part of me shall always be with her. I shall ask for her to give me a lock of her hair, and I will always wear her on my fingers as well — Darcy, I had a thought that I should make an additional one for you to give Miss Elizabeth, but I didn't have any of your hair with me."

Thank God.

Darcy was no enthusiast for the modern practice of sticking hair into rings. It was romantic, yes, but... hair belonged on the head, not in a ring or locket. It was an irrational preference, but he was allowed to have such preferences.

Like his equally irrational preference for Elizabeth Bennet.

Miss Bingley screeched out, "No! No. No. No. No. No. You are not marrying Miss Bennet."

"Yes I am."

"You can't marry her. I don't want you to, and this is not a choice that you can make without considering me and Louisa and Mr. Hurst."

"Jolly good girl, and Mrs. Bennet sets a fine table. You can marry her with my blessings, not that you give a tuppence for them," Mr. Hurst said. Darcy had quite forgotten the presence of the man, as he had watched Bingley's puppylike enthusiasm.

"Fine! Then consider me and Louisa."

Mrs. Hurst looked between her husband and her sister, clearly unsure who she was supposed to side with in a case where they disagreed. Mr. Hurst took Mrs. Hurst's arm. "Capital idea though, making a ring with hair in it. Capital idea, I'll have a lock of mine sent off to your jeweler in London and he can make one for Louisa to wear. Should be ready in time for your wedding. Which is not detrimental to Louisa's interests either." Mr. Hurst winked and said to Miss Bingley, "Can't forget, Jane is going to be Mr. Darcy's sister."

Then with a further comment about the conversation boring him, and that he needed a nap, and his wife's presence during said nap, Mr. Hurst left the room dragging Mrs. Hurst who shrugged and looked apologetically at Miss Bingley.

Bingley shuddered. "I hate when Mr. Hurst does that. I know exactly what they are going to be doing in five minutes. And with my *sister*. Can't he be more discreet?"

Miss Bingley blinked confusedly. "Whatever are you talking about?"

Bingley smiled benignly on her. "Tis best you do not know."

"You can't marry Jane." She said it again, but something of her fire had been drained by having much of her expected support leave like that.

"Why ever not? What is wrong with her?"

"*Everything.* But mainly her sisters. Miss Elizabeth is a... a low, dishonest chit. She's practically a... a strumpet!"

"Caroline!" Bingley gasped shocked at what his sister had said.

Miss Bingley squeaked and paled, she looked between Darcy and Colonel Fitzwilliam.

"Miss Bingley, I must demand an apology for this insult against *my* future wife."

Darcy's glare cowed the woman this time. And Miss Bingley knew that her overstepped her bounds. "I... I am overtaken by passion for my brother's interests. So I overstepped my bounds. I ought not have said that."

Darcy continued to glare at her. He began to become authentically angry. She had practically accused Elizabeth of being a woman of ill repute, and him in turn of being the sort of man who would throw his entire fortune upon such a woman.

Miss Bingley flushed deeper. "I apologize."

"Do you?"

"Congratulations again." Bingley exclaimed to break the tension. "Darcy. Congratulations. I have not said it enough times. And I'm deuced pleased, man, that you decided to marry her. Know you must have had reservations about her connections, coming from Pemberley and all. The whole Darcy name. But I am proud of you for doing the reasonable thing, only reasonable thing, and marrying Miss Elizabeth."

Darcy wryly returned Bingley's smile, almost feeling happy.

"You can't let them win again!" Caroline exclaimed, apparently not sufficiently cowed. "They already snagged one rich man, and—"

"Really, Caro, it isn't about money. It is about love."

"Of course it is about *money*. It is the only reason anyone ever likes us."

Bingley blinked at that. Then he grinned. "Darcy, dear fellow. You only like me for my money?"

"No."

Bingley grinned and tilted his head. "Are you sure? I mean, since you have so *little* money yourself, you want to be near such a grand fortune as I have."

Darcy grunted. "You are easy to like. For many reasons."

"Ha! Caroline, you *used to* agree with everything Darcy said. I'd imagine you won't now though, since you can't hope to marry him."

Miss Bingley growled in frustration at her brother. It looked like she wanted to leap on him and attack him.

The time had come for Darcy to take the lead, since any hope of getting Bingley to see reason would go right out the window if Miss Bingley kept at him in this way. "Miss Bingley, leave. I would speak with your brother alone. Perhaps I might convince him..."

"No! You have already been fooled by this family once; I'll not have additional damage done to us by your pathetic weakness for Bennet women. You'll—"

"Really, Caro," Bingley said calmly, "you cannot speak to Mr. Darcy in this way."

"Fine! Marry Jane Bennet! You will be miserable with just her company to make you happy. My position will be hurt — can you not think of *me*? For just *once* in your life think about someone besides yourself."

"I have often thought of you, Caroline. And often done things for you, like the money I lent you last month. For those extra dresses you insisted you needed."

"Zounds! You infuriate me — you are determined upon ruining us in the face of the world, you will provide me with a terrifically terrible set of connections to Mrs. Bennet and her brood of disgraceful—"

"You seem bitter."

"Just marry her, and I will *sneer* and laugh when you are miserable."

Miss Bingley mercifully left the room.

Shaking his head, Bingley walked to the sideboard and poured himself a thick tumbler of brandy. "Did not enjoy that." He tossed it back, and then poured a second glass to sip. He gestured to both of the gentlemen left in the room in question. Darcy shook his head, he needed his wits about him, while Colonel Fitzwilliam happily strode forward to collect the glass Bingley poured for him.

Bingley added again, "Did not enjoy facing her like that at all."

"Did a passable job of it," Colonel Fitzwilliam replied. "Decidedly passable."

Bingley made a face, and sipped the cognac. "Is that a compliment or an insult?"

"Too mediocre for either. *My* sisters understood that there were matters they could not attack me upon many years ago. When I was much younger than you are. But different types. Different types."

"I hate to argue, or to disappoint anyone. It feels almost physically painful to know that she is angry at me. But so it must be, and I must make clear to her I will tolerate no insult against Jane or her family. None. What I'm surprised at, Darcy, is that *you* did not step in to defend them more strongly. She is your sister. Your mother. Will be anyway."

Darcy grimaced. Great. He already was settled by the world, by his dearest friend, as belonging with Mrs. Bennet, and he was already expected to force the whole world to respect and admire the unadmirable and unrespectable.

He could see them in London — he'd do his best to tell them they could not camp in his townhouse, or presume upon his name, but like Mr. Collins had introduced himself, as his aunt's clergyman, Lydia and Mrs. Bennet — especially those two — would approach every duke and earl in Hyde Park, even the ones Darcy had never drummed up acquaintance with — and say, "Yo good fellow! Are you a single man of large fortune in want of a wife? Darcy, you know Darcy, he is my dear, dear son, so I do not need to stand on ceremony with any man in England. Well, do you want a wife? Lydia here will do finely for you."

And Lydia would prance, and simper, and then exclaim, "He isn't wearing a red coat, I don't care how many titles he has, he isn't worth my time."

And *that* was what Elizabeth had brought him to with her scheme to force him to marry her.

Never forget.

Even if he *also* was to never again mention it, or even think of it in her presence. Since he *did* want a passionate and happy marriage.

"Darcy! *Darcy.*" The combined voices of Bingley and Colonel Fitzwilliam broke him from his reverie.

Bingley chuckled, "You looked as though a ghost had just attacked you. What were you thinking upon?"

"Bingley, you must drop this plan to marry Miss Bennet."

Bingley's face got a mulish growl. "Not good enough for your sister. Huh. Just because my wealth is from trade. Well I won't do it. I won't drop her. I saw her first. *You* said Lizzy wasn't even handsome enough to tempt you, and now we've all seen how tempting you find her. Well Jane is my angel, and you can't take her from me."

Colonel Fitzwilliam had the overwide smile of a Cheshire cat, and he silently laughed at Darcy like a loon, as Darcy exclaimed, "No! No! That is not it at all! Not at all. I'd happily let you marry my sister. Georgiana, that is. If you wanted. I don't stand on any such ceremony. Nothing could delight me more than to be your brother."

Bingley grinned, like the sun had burst forth from the clouds, lighting up the ground with a beam of light. "You do! And we shall be brothers!"

"Jane is not... she is not worthy of your admiration. Her family is below yours. And—"

"Darcy, what are you talking about? You are going to be her brother. I am — talk sense, man. I am not so clever as you, and what you say makes no sense. If you thought that, you never would have offered to marry Miss Elizabeth — deuced glad you did. You two are perfect for each—"

"I never did!"

Damn Colonel Fitzwilliam and that grin. If it got any wider, the top of his head would fall off.

"She tricked me. She arranged for me to be obliged to marry her, and

Jane is a fortune hunter of the same sort."

"What are you talking about? How did Elizabeth trick—" Then Bingley shook his head and laughed. "You lay it on quite thick, but I *saw* you two. Caught up in as pretty of a kiss as I've ever seen, your tongue three inches down her throat, and your hands—"

"Enough! No descriptions," Darcy shouted as Colonel Fitzwilliam cackled like a mad witch.

Bingley shrugged. "Don't know what you are playing at, but you can't pretend you don't have quite the passion for Miss Elizabeth. Not after *that* kiss."

"I *am* passionately attached to her, but I never would have offered for her if I had not been obliged to by the situation."

"That," Colonel Fitzwilliam quipped, "speaks very ill of both your sense and sensibility."

"She timed it with her mother, so that you and Sir William would be brought there to witness us, right as we were kissing."

Bingley blinked at this information. "Mrs. Bennet seemed quite surprised."

"She was *playing a part*. And she fooled *you*."

"A good part — she had been discoursing but a minute before on how much she disliked you, and how much superior I was in person and manners to you. It was a *quick* turnaround." Bingley grinned. "But I don't mind hearing you good naturedly roasted, not when you deserve it."

"It was all part of the scheme to entrap me!"

"Mr. Darcy," Colonel Fitzwilliam said, "has determined to think the choice of marriage to Elizabeth is beneath his high dignity as the master of Pemberley, but as he desperately wants to marry her, he chooses to make the pretence, to himself mainly, but also to us, of believing that she tricked him, when she obviously did not, so that he does not need to face that he wants her body, soul and mind more than he wants a well-connected dowry and everything he always thought he was supposed to want."

"Oh!" Bingley nodded sensibly. "I understand *now*."

"That is not—"

"Hahahaha." Bingley grinned. "Hadn't expected *you* to be caught in such a petty self-deception. But I suppose it is not so petty. So I am going to ask Jane to marry me, and when you come to your senses, you will be very happy we are brothers."

"No!"

Bingley raised his eyebrows.

"You cannot because... she is a fortune hunter and the entire family is mercenary and counting upon making the best match they can for all of their girls. And you are being manipulated into offering for her, like I was manipulated into marriage with Elizabeth."

"Clearly not, as, to my misfortune, I am not kissing Jane at this moment."

Colonel Fitzwilliam laughed, and then tried to adopt a neutral expression at Darcy's glare. The smile was still very present on the edges.

"She does not want to marry you, but she will do as her mother tells her to — I tell you, Bingley, I observed her closely the night of the ball and since. She does not show any intense passion when your name is spoken. She simply does not care greatly for you, and you would be doing Miss Bennet an ill turn if you offered for her because she would have no choice but to do what her mother asks, and marry you."

Bingley frowned and worriedly paced while covering his mouth with his hand. Darcy was unsurprised, this hit Bingley in a point he was weak in: his sense of self-worth and self-confidence. "You surely don't think — I would not want her to marry me if she did not love me and want me. No sane man would want a woman who did not love him. But... I thought. I am sure I thought. Jane always spoke to me in such a way. In such a way. Darcy, are you certain she does not love me?"

"Balderdash!" Colonel Fitzwilliam's voice echoed, rattling the windows. The other two members of the conversation looked at him. Colonel Fitzwilliam repeated, more quietly, "Balderdash, and nonsense. Bingley, you *know* Darcy. What does he know about passion or a woman's looks? He doesn't even know *himself*, how could he know the thoughts of the delectable, and fine figured and exquisite nose possessing Jane Bennet?"

"But, if Jane does not love me, and I made her to marry—"

"Balderdash!"

"But—"

"Complete tosh! Hogwash to it! A nitwitted notion of anti-Napoleonic proportions — by which I mean very large." Seeing that he had successfully cowed Bingley into silence, Colonel Fitzwilliam said, "The elegantly fingered and angelically cheeked Miss Bennet will not marry you if she does not love you." He held up a hand to forestall any objections from Darcy. "All you have established, dear cousin, is that her mother would push her to accept the match. Children often ignore their mothers."

Colonel Fitzwilliam handed his drinking glass to Bingley, who obediently refilled it as the officer continued his discourse. "My mother has a fancy for the classics, and she wished for me to become a scholar of great renown, or an antiquarian digging out Saxon barrows like Cunnington, and to that end she made me recite in Greek the great Homeric epics before I went to sleep each evening. And look at me now." Colonel

Fitzwilliam held his hands wide, and pointed at himself with a satisfied air. "She could not be more disappointed."

"I see that," Bingley nodded and handed the glass to Colonel Fitzwilliam, who downed it immediately and handed it back.

"Thirsty work, convincing a man to be sensible and propose marriage to the very image of feminine perfection whom he loves. Let us now look upon Darcy. His mother wished him to be a sociable friendly man who could easily mix with persons of any class — it is true. I remember her saying as much many times. And look how he has turned out. Have you ever ignored your mother's wishes?"

"Well her school friend Gladys. She wanted me to marry Gladys's daughter. Said they planned the match when we were in our cradles. But Jove." Bingley shuddered. "By Jove. Darcy, you remember how that girl looked. A hideous creature. Not for my mother. Not for any cause — ohhhhh. I see. Yes. Jane would not marry me to please her mother."

"Pour for yourself some more. You deserve it."

Bingley did, and Colonel Fitzwilliam clinked his glass with him.

"You don't want to put her in the uncomfortable position of needing to refuse you," Darcy said, desperately. "And if she doesn't love you, she will refuse. And it will be uncomfortable for you too. Better, much better to just say nothing."

"Oh." Bingley's high mood evaporated once more. "Are you so sure she would refuse me?"

"Are! You! A Man!" Colonel Fitzwilliam roared into Bingley's face so hard that the young man shook and spilled his liquor onto the ground in shock. Colonel Fitzwilliam threw his hands in the air and said, "I repent of ever encouraging you towards the satin slippered and flashing eyed Miss Bennet. Such a woman. Oooooh." Colonel Fitzwilliam closed his eyes, as if in ecstasy. "Such a *woman*. She deserves a better *man* than you. A *man* who can know his own mind and act on it. A *man* who doesn't need certainty that his plans will work before he acts. By Ares, the God of War, I swear, that if she had even a mere ten thousand, I'd pursue her 'til she agreed to be mine."

That statement made Bingley's eyes widen, and him to shake his head frantically no.

"In fact," Colonel Fitzwilliam continued, warming to his subject and pacing back and forth before the window, "I shall pursue her in any case. I have ample capital set aside from victory bonuses. I can afford a wife who brings nothing. After we are married, Miss Bennet shall come with me on campaign, and stay in my tent as I smite the French with my guns and my swords and my mighty regiment. And then I shall return, bloodied from the field of battle and she shall be present awaiting me: *une femme sans vêtements!*"

As soon Colonel Fitzwilliam said this, Bingley dashed to the door and out, leaving it quivering and open. However Colonel Fitzwilliam affected a pretence that he had not noticed their host's abandoning them, and he continued to discourse in like manner until they both saw from the window Bingley on his horse dash away down the road to Longbourn at a gallop.

"Well, now you've done it," Darcy said. "He definitely is going to propose."

"Good."

"And that was an extremely improper way to speak of any gentlewoman."

"That is why I did not say it in English."

Darcy raised one skeptical eyebrow, and in a rare case of ability to be shamed, Colonel Fitzwilliam blushed.

Chapter Nine

Elizabeth was very pleased for Jane when they saw Bingley ride up to the house at a gallop. He'd returned from London and come almost immediately to see them. He leapt off the horse, and though it was distant, Elizabeth thought his hair looked surprisingly disordered by the wind. Then he was gone from their view, hidden by the overhanging gable over the front door, though the knock echoed up to the upstairs drawing room they sat in.

Not a minute later Bingley burst into the drawing room, not waiting for the butler to announce him. Mrs. Bennet began to speak greetings and effusions on her happiness at seeing Bingley's arrival.

Bingley ignored her, darted his head around wildly, and then rushed to Jane the instant he saw her. He threw himself on his knees before her and took her hands. Jane blushed but looked at him steadily, with a panting sweetness.

"Please, I love you, I adore you, you are my heart, I do not know if you love me, but though I cannot be sure, I must ask you and beg you. Say you'll marry me! Please. We would be happy. And answer quickly! He might be behind me."

"Who?"

"Colonel Fitzwilliam!"

"What has he to do with it?"

"He'll speak to you — he will somehow convince you that you want to follow him in a cold tent from field to field in the French countryside, always waiting for him to engage in a furious battle of love with you, *without any clothes!*"

"Bingley..."

The wild look in his eyes faded. "You don't want to marry Colonel Fitzwilliam?"

"No, he rather scares me." Jane tilted her head to look at Bingley. "You do love me. Oh I am so happy! Yes! Yes! A thousand times yes, I will marry you. I have barely let myself to hope…" She said softly, "I love you. It is you I love. Only you. Oh, you have made me so happy."

And then, in front of the family, they kissed softly and sweetly, before Jane realized they were all watching and blushingly they stopped and grinned to receive congratulations.

Some time later Elizabeth asked Mr. Bingley while she sat as a chaperone with him and Jane, "What *did* Colonel Fitzwilliam have to do with anything?" She had given them thirty minutes to kiss and fondle (chastely, of course, nothing like how she and Darcy kissed and fondled) before her curiosity overcame her and she asked directly.

"Ah, he was — he wanted to ensure that I was worthy of Jane, and that I would ask her to marry her."

"I still do not see how the matter was any business of his — though if you needed the support from your friends to fortify you in making a proposal… I suppose that is forgivable."

"I should not. A man does not need certainty, he only must know his own wishes, and my wishes are for the slim waisted and silk garbed Jane Bennet — Jove, no! I don't want to talk like him."

Jane blushed. "That is a very pretty sentiment."

"I love you, Jane, you are my angel. You are my dear, you are the one who I adore from the bottom of my feet to the tip of my hair. But I shall not speak to you in the convoluted way of Colonel Fitzwilliam."

She giggled. "But you just did."

"In any case, Mr. Darcy tried to dissuade me from offering."

"Mr. Darcy. *My betrothed*. He tried to keep you from marrying Jane. My sister. My sister who loves you."

Bingley raised his hands defensively. "Now do not be angry with him, he only wished to protect me — and Jane too — you see he worried Jane would only accept me because your mother wanted her to and—"

"I am certain *that* was not his real worry."

Bingley froze. His eyes went wide like a hunted thing. "Don't make me say mean things about my dearest friend. He is really a good man. Really. Really. And despite what he says he loves you."

"Me, now! What does he say about *me*?"

"Uh. It would be best, I judge, if I say nothing."

"What. Did. He. Say."

"He just insisted that you are a fortune hunter who tricked him into being forced to marry you, but... but—"

"He insists that, does he," Elizabeth said coldly.

"Now, now," Bingley said defensively. "Do not be too angry. He only said such to me and Colonel Fitzwilliam. It was not as though my sisters were still in the room."

"That. Do you think *that* makes me feel better about the calumnies that my *betrothed* heaps upon my head?"

"My." Bingley rubbed his head. "I did not mean to get Darcy in such trouble — but he does care for you very much, and, as Colonel Fitzwilliam insists, he is filled with a burning and unquenchable passion for you, which he cannot control, and which he pretends to deny by claiming you are forcing him to marry, but none of us are fooled."

"*I* am fooled. And as I am the principle person involved — zounds!" Elizabeth threw her hands in the air. "Had I a choice about the matter, he is the last gentleman in the world whom I would choose to marry. In fact there are hundreds of thousands of men in England alone who are not gentlemen, but rather woodcutters, and gardeners and the men who collect the muck from cesspits and drag it from the cities so it can be used as fertilizer. And *if I had a choice*, I would rather marry any of them."

Bingley blinked.

Jane said softly, "Surely you don't mean *that*."

"Find me a night soil man, wearing still the clothes and stench of his trade. I'll kiss him straight away. With passion too."

"By Jove!" Bingley pointed with a shocked slack face at Elizabeth, "She is as self-deluded as Darcy is."

"I am not self-deluded."

"Are too."

"Am not."

"Are too."

"Am — Bingley! This is a child's game."

Bingley grinned and stuck his tongue out at Elizabeth. "Since we are to be siblings, I can act as childishly and informally with you as I want. I am delighted, and you shall be delighted as well, when you and Darcy realize at last how good of a couple you make."

"That is *not* likely to happen any time soon."

But, as the great Scots poet said, *The best-laid schemes o' Mice an' Men gang aft agley.*

Much to Elizabeth's shock, *she* would accept the full flower of her affection during the course of her conversation with Darcy about his opinions upon Jane's marriage.

*****

There was no great course of time given to Elizabeth to calm down before Mr. Darcy and Colonel Fitzwilliam called upon the Bennets at Longbourn to give their congratulations to the happy couple.

At least Colonel Fitzwilliam heartedly congratulated Mr. Bingley, made repeated remarks about the younger gentleman having stolen a march upon him, much as Wellington once stole a march upon a French marshal in the mountains of Spain, when his regiment became the thin red line which hid behind the crest of a hill and rose up to crush the French army with a hail of good solid English — and Scot, and Welsh and Irish — lead.

Darcy's congratulations were along the lines of, "I hope you shall be happy," delivered in a manner that indicated a clear belief that his friend ought not be, even if he probably would be.

With a laugh Colonel Fitzwilliam said, "From Darcy's manner, you would think he was in love with Miss Bennet rather than Miss Elizabeth."

"I am not acting in such a way."

"Then be happy for your friend who is to marry the fine ankled—"

Darcy interrupted him. "Enough on Jane Bennet's charms!"

Bingley and Jane were far enough away to not hear the comments, but Elizabeth could not imagine that Bingley would like to listen to Colonel Fitzwilliam speak so upon his betrothed.

A call went up amongst the group for them to go out on a walk. Jane and Bingley wished a chance to speak to each other without being observed by so many others. Elizabeth wished a chance to berate Mr. Darcy in private. Lydia Bennet wished a chance to flirt with Colonel Fitzwilliam, as she had spent the preceding day being sprinkled with stories from the officers of the regiment about how much they admired the man, and as a result, though she still found him barely tolerable to look at, she was convinced it would greatly impress everyone if they saw him making love to her.

Such a confluence of desires could not be denied by the cold of an English December, and thus, gloved, glowing (with happiness, anger or hope), jacketed and shawled the group exited upon their walk, each breath playing out in an icy cloud.

The groups naturally separated, Lydia talking to Colonel Fitzwilliam, who allowed her to drone on, as she became more and more annoyed with his refusal to answer as he sunk into the memories of a good day of battle during the campaign against Marshal Soult that he and his regiment were but recently returned from.

Jane and Mr. Bingley lagged all the way behind, looking with little sugary glances at each other, and glowing cheerily with love and cold cheeks.

Elizabeth and Darcy marched forward, neither saying anything to the other at first. Darcy could detect Elizabeth was angry, and he had a high enough opinion of Bingley's incautiousness in speech so as to have a good idea of what was upon her mind. He imagined what her first words would be, what the lashing question would be, considering in his heart how to argue so perfectly as to convince her that he had been doing the right, the honorable, and the moral thing, by attacking Jane.

The fact was though, Darcy felt more than a little guilt.

Jane's glow of happiness was too great for him to believe that she had been indifferent to his friend. The girl would have been heartbroken if Bingley had done the wise thing and walked away from the entanglement.

111

"Why do you *scorn* me so?"

Elizabeth's eyes were tearing up.

When Darcy looked at her in surprise, she continued, "I can't — I can't do it. Not if you hate me this way. Not if you tell everyone dear to you that you despise me and distrust me. Not if *you* distrust me in this way — what did I do to deserve this treatment?"

"What are you saying?"

"I did not try to entrap you in marriage. I did *not*. You — why do you insist on... hating me in this way."

"I do not hate you."

"You despise me. You look down on me. You think me of no moral worth. Even after we are to marry, you try to keep your friends from marrying us. You would have devastated Jane, and *why*?"

"Lizzy..."

"No!" Elizabeth sternly turned her head so she could not look at him. 'You do have the right to look at me in that way, and make me to forget the way you scorn me and my family, the way you mistreat me and those dearest to me, the way you despise me. You do. I can't — I won't marry you. I'll face the scandal. I'll... I'll face my mother, and everything else. If you hate me, I won't marry a man who hates me."

"Lizzy." Some part of Darcy's mind was aware that this was his chance to let *her* break the engagement. And if he did, because she believed him to hate her, when he did not, that would be as dishonorable as riding away himself without a word to her. "I do not hate you."

"You do! Everything you do, everything you say — you told Bingley and Colonel Fitzwilliam that I am nothing but a fortune hunter. You claimed *Jane* was also a fortune hunter, when she is all good, and all that is noble. And—"

"I chiefly claimed to Bingley that your sister did not love him. Which I see now was false, but I spoke from an honest conviction."

"Like you speak from an honest conviction when you call me a fortune hunter?"

Fitzwilliam Darcy at that moment, and for the first time, truly *doubted* his assumption that she had trapped him. Her passion and pain were too pointed.

"I…" Darcy covered his mouth.

"But forget me — what place is it for you to manage Bingley's life. For you to destroy his happiness and that of my sister? Is it *spite*? You are so angry at me, that you are determined to hurt Jane because I care for her?"

Darcy ground his jaw. "That is a low accusation."

"It shows a higher opinion of *you* that you have of me."

"I never… did you, did you honestly try to trap me?"

Elizabeth did not deign to reply.

"I do have reasons to believe a marriage into your family is a poorly chosen marriage. To counsel Bingley that he had best not to marry one of you. Reasons beyond…" Darcy stuttered to a stop. He tried to take Elizabeth's arm, but she would not let him touch her. "Perhaps I am wrong."

"About what?"

"You. Whether you—"

"*Perhaps*? You, wrong? *You* never could be wrong. I, knowing my own memories, *knowing* that my mother could not count to *ten* in time with another person, have begun to suspect I am a fortune hunter, simply because the damned almighty Fitzwilliam Darcy can never, ever be bloody wrong!"

Elizabeth stood stiffly, beautifully away from him. A vein pulsed in her neck. She crossed her arms and turned away from him.

He tried to touch her shoulder, to draw her to him, so he could try to kiss her or embrace her again. She flinched away, and stepped outside of his reach.

She was beautiful, he wanted her.

"So why, what other reason could you have to council against my sister?" When Darcy hesitated she snapped, "*Speak.*"

"Your mother and your sisters — and also a little your father. During the night of the ball, I saw the spectacle they made of themselves. Miss Lydia running in circles drunk, waving an officer's sword. Miss Mary, having no notion that she had overstayed her welcome at the piano — I do not complain that she attempted to display when her abilities were not up to the task, but why did your parents never teach her to only attempt one, or at the most two, songs in a night? And your *mother*. I heard her speaking loud and clear about how she had won for herself a rich husband. She was dividing Bingley's wealth upon herself quite as neatly as if it were her own deserved inheritance. And you wonder why I wished to protect my friend from such a family? Why I wondered at the motives of this family?"

Elizabeth blushed and blushed. She could not defend her mother. She had tried to silence her. She could not defend her sisters. She could not defend her father. She felt all of the shame of the connection.

"Next to this," Darcy said, "the disgrace of connections to trade and to a country lawyer — which cannot be of nearly so great an objection to Bingley as to me — are of small consideration. Your family shall disgrace any they are connected to. I fully expect they shall disgrace me."

Tears started breaking out on Elizabeth's face. She hurt inside. And she did not even know why. She hated Darcy, even if she had to marry him, she hated him. Even if she usually wanted to kiss him, she hated him. The desire, even now the desire she felt for his clean shaven cheeks and to run her fingers over his thick eyebrows made her to hurt.

Suddenly he looked at her. He really looked at her, his eyes intent upon her, almost as if he were looking at her for the first time.

His hand reached forward hesitatingly. It paused almost at her cheeks. Then he touched her softly, and against her own wishes, for she wished to be proud and stiff, and stand away from him, she leaned into his gloved hand as he brushed the icy tears from her half numb face. "I..."

He trailed off. His eyes caressed her. And his hand too.

She tried desperately to hold back the tears. She shouldn't sob in front of him, and she didn't know why she wanted to. She had always known everything he said about her family was true.

"You have..." Darcy swallowed. "You never did try to trap me, did you?"

She mutely shook her head. "I thought you despised me, and that I despised you. I never, never..."

"I... I have wronged you."

"You did. It... it is... *ungentlemanly* to throw my family's defects at me. *Don't you think I know?*"

He nodded silently.

His gloves softly caressed her cheeks, and he looked like he wanted to kiss her. Instead he put one of his long, strong arms around her back and held her against him. This time Elizabeth did not resist. She couldn't help herself and began sobbing against the fine wool of his coat on his chest. Mr. Darcy smelled very good. "We aren't bad people. We aren't. We don't deserve this scorn."

"You do not deserve any scorn," Darcy echoed her. He held her against him, stroking his hand down her back, and she relaxed into his tall body. He kissed the top of her head.

"I never did it. I always, always meant to marry only if I had some love. Some attachment. And I would never bring a man to marry me who didn't wish to marry me. Not what I wanted. It isn't."

"Lizzy." He spoke softly into her hair. His body was warm in the cold afternoon wind, and his coat smelled like him when she kissed him. And she was beginning to calm down. It terrified her that she needed Darcy's comfort, even when he had been the one to enrage and hurt her.

"I don't *care* how much pin money, or how large Pemberley is, or *any of that rot*. Not if you... not if you despise me. I won't go through with it. I won't."

"I don't despise you. I... I truly admire you. You didn't trap me. You are too honest and good to do so, I see that now..."

"My aunt and uncle. The ones you haven't met. My mother's brother. A good man. Well bred, intelligent, and caring. A *good* man. Nothing like Mama. I'm scared. You'll, you'll... you despise connections with trade so much, and because... because..." She glared at Darcy again. "I love my family, and *I never wanted this.* I didn't trap you. I didn't. It was an accident. That *damned* rug. Its fault." Elizabeth sniffled into his coat, leaving snot and tears on the green dyed wool, and not caring because he deserved it, everything. "That damned rug."

"Yes," Darcy whispered in reply. "The damned rug."

"Not me."

"Never you."

"Not *me*."

"I think... I think that I knew always. Elizabeth, can you ever forgive me for doubting you? I would wish… I would wish, since we must marry, for us to have a friendly… a happy marriage. In all ways. Not just passionate, but companionate — you are too good. You are too good to have trapped me."

"*Jane* never would have agreed to marry Bingley if she didn't love him."

Elizabeth could feel in Darcy's body some tension that she knew meant he didn't agree with her. "She *wouldn't* have."

Darcy kissed her hair again. And her forehead. "I only guess. You know your sister. But I know you, and I know *you* would never have acted as I expected Jane to act."

"I wouldn't have. Never."

"I swear, no matter what I think of their manners, I will dine as equals with any of your family. I have been wrong, I am heartily ashamed to think of how I have thought, while planning to marry you. I have been wrong to do so, and I shall treat your family as I would treat the family of a duke, were I to marry his daughter."

"Good." Elizabeth looked at him, she was sure her face was blotchy and red from the tears. She sniffled again. With a quiet smile he handed her his handkerchief. She took the fine silk, with FD embroidered in the corner and blew her nose into it.

Darcy put his hand around the back of her head and softly pulled her forward, and they kissed, slowly instead of passionately. But Elizabeth liked it more, because she hoped, she thought, that they might be in tune one with the other. And for the first time she honestly felt hopeful, and almost, though not quite, glad that she was to marry Fitzwilliam Darcy.

After some minutes they realized they were entirely alone along a wooded path. Elizabeth shivered from the cold from standing still for so long, and by mutual agreement they vigorously walked together, with

Darcy smilingly leading her with his long strides. Such a completely handsome man.

Elizabeth had good reason to be generally considered a lucky woman.

After such a discussion it was impossible for some minutes for them to speak at all. They walked through coppiced woods, past a grove of free growing oaks, and across two further fields and had reached halfway to Oakham mount, before they began to speak again, upon light matters at first.

They argued amiably about a line of news in the day's paper regarding the price of wheat, Darcy asked Elizabeth about the books that she had purchased the previous day, when he met her with Colonel Fitzwilliam, and Elizabeth confessed her mind had been too full for her to settle upon reading it all evening, but she had looked at, and admired the prints of several Rembrandts with great admiration.

And Darcy talked about his visits to the collections of wealthy friends, and the Rembrandts he had seen, but he himself, while he had two Reubens and an allegorical scene by Brueghel the Elder, he had none of the paintings of that great master. "In frankness, the Darcy nature has been to focus upon the collection of books more than that of paintings. In this preference I share. And even amongst books, we have a preference for a breadth of books above the earliest and rarest editions and copies. Though we do have a first edition folio of Shakespeare, and we have kept the originals of letters that Queen Elizabeth wrote to a Darcy ancestor during her reign."

"Your family goes back so far?"

"We do — though the letters went to an earl whose male line died out during the Civil War, and whose surviving daughter married my great grandfather, six or seven generations back."

"Oh, and did the Darcys stand with Bonny Charlie or with Cromwell?"

Darcy grinned. "I must confess the Darcy family made no effort to cover itself with glory during those days. We had members who fought both for the long parliament, and for the king, in undistinguished roles. The head of the family during the day made an effort to keep from paying taxes or raising troops for the other side, and he was quite ready to proclaim loyalty to whichever side was winning at the time."

"I cannot imagine *you* behaving in such a manner."

Darcy shrugged. "Neither can I. But our holdings and fortune doubled during that time, so he was a successful lord, and he cared for the wellbeing of his retainers and family, even if he sided with neither side in the great conflict. For myself, my inclinations are to despise both Tories and the Whigs. Cromwell murdered his true Lord and King, while that Lord and King wished to turn those subjects from free men to slaves like those of the French King. And again, I despise the revolutionaries *there* for murdering their king, and I despise their king for deserving to be murdered."

"You wish to live in a better world?"

"I wish to fulfill mine own obligations, to those who depend upon me, and let those who are disconnected from my affection and my position manage as they might. I am a man loyal to King George and to the crown prince. But I am very glad that whatever the defects of our royal family today — I am not blind to the deficiencies in matters of morality and judgement that they possess — they are made of sounder stuff than Charles the first was. I am glad I can give my loyalty to those men without reserve. And I think I can understand the choices of James Darcy of the Civil War. I do not know I would have done differently if faced between the choice of supporting rebellion or supporting the destruction of our constitution."

"I begin to understand you." Elizabeth smiled at Darcy.

"Do you? I feel myself, on this matter, without a deep understanding of myself." He grinned at her. "Perhaps, you shall interpret me to me."

"It is very much like you, to see a wisdom in both sides." Elizabeth smirked impishly. "And to despise both for their failings. I did once tell you that you had a propensity to hate everyone."

Darcy laughed. "It is strange that I can find amusement in this. It is your manner in saying such a thing."

"Of *course* it is. One's *words* are at most half of a communication. Tone, meaning, the situation. Does that surprise you? I am happy at this moment, but I am not blind to your faults."

"You mean to indicate you do not see me as entirely flawless and faultless? And I had so hoped to marry a woman who would feed my every ego."

Elizabeth worked her eyebrows in a weird and frustrated waggle. Giving up, she sighed explosively, "Zounds! I want to be able to lift just the one eyebrow as you do."

Darcy laughed again, and added, "I shall try to not be blind to my faults either."

Some gusts of wind, and the realization that they had lost both the pair of Bingley and Jane and Colonel Fitzwilliam and Lydia led them to determine to turn back towards Longbourn.

"Your cousin. I wonder how he does with my sister."

"Are you worried for him, or for Lydia?"

"Oh! Very much for Lydia."

"I do not think he shall eat her, no matter how nicely she speaks of Wickham."

"Oh, it is quite the opposite. The officers have determined they despise Mr. Wickham, and while she is quite brave enough to take up his case in despite of *you*, to stand her ground in the face of a general social disapproval is quite beyond her talents. No, she is hopeful of impressing the other officers by being seen speaking to a man who they have determined to admire. Apparently stories about how impressive Colonel Fitzwilliam is have been circulating in the mess halls. It appears he earned a notable reputation on the Peninsula."

"A deserved one."

"He is… very much an officer. And a gentleman. And a… well whatever it is that he is, he is an exemplary version of it."

"Yes." Darcy nodded and smiled dryly. "He is very much so."

"And a good man. The story of him going after Rattail, I mean Wickham — do not laugh. It is quite serious to become confused upon a man's name. Wickham's name should be associated with candles and bacon, not with — I told you not to laugh."

Darcy snorted. "Candlebacon — you should tell that one to Richard."

"And I shall. He is a man who can appreciate a lively joke. Not handsome, but yet…"

"Compelling."

"Yes. That is a good word. Intense. Very… manly. I fear for the French, with him in the army."

Darcy nodded. "And his manners with the ladies are less… intense than amongst men. He never lacks for female company, nor words to say amongst them. He and I are different in that way. I have not his easiness with strangers, his skill for catching the interests of a new acquaintance, and making it to seem as though I care for them as well as they care for themselves."

"Is this an apology upon how you entered our neighborhood and in one night managed to offend everyone at once?" Elizabeth smiled flirtatiously at him. "Well?"

"Mayhap. An excuse perhaps — which ought to be beneath me. Perhaps I treat others as being beneath me, since it gives me an excuse to not treat with them at all, and that is my true goal."

"A self-confessed misanthrope!" Elizabeth smiled happily. "But I know you better than you know yourself. Or I hope to. I believe I have gotten a grip on the true passion that drives you: not a disdain for the company of other men, but shyness. Underneath that harsh, compelling, and quite cold exterior are friendly thoughts towards all mankind, and a simple desire to communicate."

"That is not quite accurate — though a flattering picture. Perhaps I am... shy. But I fear beneath the disinclination to put myself to the trouble of overcoming that shyness is a disinclination to believe it would be worthwhile for me to do so."

"That does not make you a misanthrope, just ignorant of the true pleasures to be found in communion betwixt people."

Darcy grinned back at her. It made something glow inside her stomach. They took each other's arms again, and continued along the country road, the cold which flapped through their coats could not dim the growing warmth in Elizabeth's belly.

"I sometimes feel," Darcy said slowly, hesitatingly, "less next to my cousin. He has not a fraction of my wealth, and I know his appearance is not so well remarked upon as mine, yet he is so..." Darcy trailed off.

Elizabeth laughed merrily. "Women are not so shallow as to only look at a man's appearance. If you *must* choose a man to mark yourself wanting next to, Colonel Fitzwilliam is a far better choice than Mr. Wickham."

"You thought I compared myself to Mr. Wickham and found myself wanting?"

"You *are* wanting in matters of charm — though not in essentials. In essentials you are much superior to Mr. Wickham, and much more to *my* liking than Colonel Fitzwilliam. You need not feel jealousy towards either man when around me, on my part *your* handsome features and sensible mind, and stable character are much preferred. Mr. Candlebacon we can simply dismiss. He has no more substance than a candle's flame, able to burn a moth, but not much more. As for your cousin..."

Elizabeth's mouth twisted. How could she reassure Darcy that he was superior to his cousin, without at the same time appearing to insult Colonel Fitzwilliam in any way?

"Yes?" Darcy prodded her, his face open and calm, but with that hint of a mischievous smile lurking at the corner.

"You see my problem!"

"Surely you can compliment me in some way."

"Then *that* is what I shall do. You are sensible, informed on a broad range of topics, self-controlled, in most matters, and yet passionate and driven by your sense of right and you are... ah, driven by your passionate emotions when proper—"

"There was nothing proper about—"

"No. No. Do not say what you mean to. A woman *likes* when a gentleman cannot be gentlemanly around *her* charms. So long as he is reserved enough when she wishes him to be."

"Ah." That mischievous smile was growing. "I too, admire when a woman, who usually is a model of propriety, can be overcome by the strength of her passions, so far as to even kiss a gentleman towards whom she feels a..."

"A decided preference. And your lips — I like them far more than Colonel Fitzwilliam's though his lips are—"

"By Saint George! I do not want to hear in detail what my future *wife* thinks about Richard's lips. No matter what the details."

"Then I shall simply say I much prefer the thought of kissing yours. Kissing the lips of any other gentleman would feel entirely wrong, while I feel quite natural, and almost proper when I kiss you." And with that Elizabeth presented her sparkling face and puffed forward lips to him.

A wise and sensible man, Darcy took the invitation and there, on the road, they kissed again.

Elizabeth found herself more and more liking the idea of their marriage and looking forward to the wedding night. Yes, especially to that. She liked how Darcy described her, a model of propriety, except for when a passion for this man — her man — overtook her.

Chapter Ten

A week before the wedding Mr. Darcy's uncle and aunt, the Earl and his wife, arrived with Darcy's sister from London. Colonel Fitzwilliam had returned to London for duties related to his regiment, but he would arrive back in Meryton the day before the wedding, along with Elizabeth's dearest relatives, Mr. and Mrs. Gardiner, who were arriving for their usual Christmas visit to Longbourn this year, while Elizabeth would be leaving for London and her honeymoon to spend Christmas with only Darcy.

The honeymoon was a prospect Elizabeth decidedly liked.

It surprised Elizabeth when Darcy's uncle, *the earl,* arrived. Darcy had suggested that the disapproval of his family was such that while they would tactfully show no public disapproval of their marriage, the lowness of her connections was such that his high born Fitzwilliam relations would refuse to provide such a strong signal of support to their low marrying nephew as to actually attend the wedding.

Now here they were.

Darcy called at Longbourn with Miss Darcy, and Lord and Lady Matlock the afternoon after they arrived. Both Elizabeth and Mrs. Bennet were in flutters of nerves. Elizabeth knew how much Mr. Darcy cared for Georgiana, and how important she was. Despite being assured that Georgiana would love her, Elizabeth also wanted to be *liked* by the younger girl.

Mrs. Bennet experienced a yet profounder flutter of nerves than her daughter. An *earl* was about to be under her roof.

For those who do not understand the significance of this, I must repeat: *An earl.*

Colonel Fitzwilliam was one thing. *He* had never intimidated her when he called upon them with Darcy. Colonel Fitzwilliam was a third son, and an officer — both groups that did not have an excess of grandeur in Mrs. Bennet's eyes. She *would* have happily seen either Kitty or Lydia marry him. Unfortunately neither of the girls had been willing to put themselves out to trap a gentleman, not like Lizzy and Jane, her cleverest daughters.

It had been a surprise to them all. Darcy had ridden in the morning the previous day to London, and now he returned with his high relatives.

When the visitors were presented to them in the drawing room, Elizabeth's eyes were first drawn to Darcy's sister. She was tall and gangly, almost coltish. She had wide sweet eyes and a nervous smile. She seemingly tried to hide behind Darcy to avoid all of the eyes looking on her. Darcy had told Elizabeth that Georgiana was a shy, sweet girl, and Elizabeth had every intention putting her at comfort.

"So." Lord Matlock spoke with a rolling voice that was similar to his youngest son's, "So, you are the girl who impressed my son so much."

Elizabeth smiled at the Lord and made a small curtsey. "As you see me."

"Hmmph." He looked her over critically and Elizabeth consciously made herself to stand taller and stare back at the man during his examination. She thought he bore the nobility of the position better than she had expected he would. There was something of grandeur and seriousness in his sharp eyes, and well-groomed bald fringe, beyond simply having expensive clothing and several thick rings upon his fingers. "I suppose. I see why Richard was impressed. Not an easy man to impress. But what a man. I sometimes wish it had been he who was my eldest... ah but it is for the best, for England, that he has been where he has been. If just Darcy sung your praises, I never would have listened to them."

"Colonel Fitzwilliam," Elizabeth agreed with a smile, "is an impressive and robust creature. I would listen intently to his words as well."

"Ha." The earl grinned at her, softening his seriousness. "Hear, hear. I'll like any girl who my nephew is willing to marry, and who my son approves of." He stuck his hand out. "Welcome to the family, Miss Elizabeth. Welcome."

Elizabeth could not help grinning back with an unexpected happiness at this approval. "Thank you. I am very glad. I shall do my utmost to keep Mr. Darcy happy."

"Good."

Darcy brought his sister forward, who could barely look at Elizabeth but when Darcy prompted her she looked up and curtseyed. Elizabeth curtseyed back smiling at her encouragingly as the introduction was made. "I have four sisters," Elizabeth said, "and I shall be very glad to have you as another."

"Oh yes! And Fitzwilliam says so much good about you. And cousin Richard as well. I hope you shall like me."

"I know I shall."

Lord Matlock looked around for a seat, and then with a courtly gesture indicated to the ladies in the room that they should all sit. He lowered himself into his seat as they did. "Too old to stand around pointless like anymore — I can never, no matter how arthritic my knees are, just cannot sit whilst a woman yet stands. Would never feel right. Don't try too hard to keep Darcy happy. The man can be morose. Not your fault if it happens. Nothing like my sister was. She was a happy woman. Friendly and kindly to everyone. A sweeter girl never existed. Mr. Darcy — his father," the Earl added gesturing at Darcy to indicate whose father he spoke of though it was obvious, "a morose fellow. Never recovered from Anne's death. Took him to his grave, the heartache did. I swear. Poor man. But he had capabilities. More intelligent than me, and with that bearing. You'd think he was a duke, or a king with the way he held himself. Always admired him, and thought it was the best thing Anne could have ever done attaching him. They were happy. Very happy. A pity they died so young."

"How old was your sister?"

"Ah. Darcy hasn't told you?" The older man glared at his nephew who looked down.

"I find it— That it is a difficult time to speak of."

"Of course it is! I remember how much you loved your mother. And your father too. But she is to be your wife. The deuce. The one person you should tell everything to." He looked at Lady Matlock who followed the conversation with sharp, thinking eyes. "I tell you everything?"

"Everything, my dear." She smiled at Elizabeth. "I think you will do for Darcy." She looked around at Longbourn's drawing room in a manner which simultaneously judged its cheapness and its taste and found both wanting. "*You* are a fine appearing girl."

"Thank you, my Lady." Elizabeth inclined her head.

The Lady smiled, a little coldly.

"Not a pleasant time," Lord Matlock spoke again. "Not for me either. Anne was just forty. Only just reached the age. Carriage accident. And—" He shivered. "She lived four days, and suffered horribly the entire time, despite the laudanum. She insisted the doctors keep her alive long enough that Fitzwilliam could return home from university to make a parting. It was a raw will she showed when she must. Horribly mangled, with no hope. If she'd been a horse, we would have shot her soon as we saw the wound to spare her the suffering. I sometimes wish…"

Elizabeth looked at Darcy. He had sat next to her, and he looked at her, and she could see the pain of the memory in his eyes. Impulsively Elizabeth took Darcy's hand. She was aware of an approving smile from Lady Matlock, but she did not care.

Darcy sighed and gripped her hand back.

"It was hard. I always adored my little sister. Ten years passed now, and yet I remember the day like yesterday — when I first saw her twisted, mangled, raw..." He shivered. "I never ride in a carriage if I can avoid it anymore. Always make sure ours has the best maintenance. And no wild horses."

Lady Matlock touched her husband's arm, and said something to him in a low voice that Elizabeth could not hear. Lord Matlock nodded. "Things happen. They just happen. We live, and find the joy we can. It is the necessity of death which makes life worth living. There is an extra intensity in taste and feeling, when you remember that suddenly you can be torn screaming in pain from the world. This is why Richard is the way he is. But damn. I wish I had not seen my little sister go like that."

Elizabeth squeezed Darcy's hand again, who gripped her hand in return so tightly the bones almost squeezed together. She had not realized this pain in Darcy's life.

"I see you comforting him." Lord Matlock smiled benevolently on them. "Richard *is* right that your marriage will be a good. Despite the natural reasons for hesitance, it *will* be a good."

Darcy said in a clipped voice, "I know you are curious, Lizzy, and my uncle will say nothing more about it. My father followed three years later. Stroke, not heartbreak, though he was heartbroken. They were happy together. Very."

She squeezed his hand again.

"Everyone says heartbreak." Darcy added, "As though that makes it *good* that he died. And the talk about how fortunate I am to have control of the estate at such a young age, when most men of my station are uselessly gambling about London with no occupation."

"And so you are." Mrs. Bennet had been silent in awe of the earl until now, but she needed to remind them all of her presence in the worst possible way. "It is a very grand thing to have possession of an estate at such a young age. My Mr. Bennet was past thirty when he assumed the estate, and living on the allowance with several daughters put me to no end of annoyance, and…"

Something in the way Darcy glared back at her made Mrs. Bennet pale and actually fall silent.

Elizabeth flushed with a weird pain and embarrassment. At this moment she hated her family, and she approved of every ill thing Darcy had said against them to Bingley. How could Mama be *so* thoughtless?

"I would much have *preferred* to have still *today. Alive. My Father.* For I loved him. And he loved me. And he would *not* have abandoned me and Georgiana — Georgiana was only ten years of age. *Ten years.* What sort of man would choose to abandon a child at that age? God chooses. God. Chooses. And we must live the test he gives us. Perhaps God's choice was a kindness to my father, for he was heartbroken. But *he* never chose to leave us."

Elizabeth was filled in her heart with sympathy for Darcy.

Everyone was quiet.

Then Darcy stood and smiled at Elizabeth. And she knew he did not hold anything her mother had said against her. "Come, I wish us to all take another walk, and we can show Georgie some of those sights you have been showing me, since we have been cramped in a carriage all day, and while cold, the day is clear and sunny, and a fine day for walking."

Over the course of the return visit the next morning, Elizabeth and Georgiana became the dearest of friends. The gentlemen went off for shooting, with Mr. Bennet and the earl joining the usual party of Bingley and Darcy. So it was just the women left alone, and as Miss Bingley now largely pretended the Bennets did not exist, Elizabeth had ample chance to charm Georgiana — with the help of the young lady's companion, Mrs. Annesley — out of her shyness.

They closeted together in the library for nearly an hour — Elizabeth had decided she liked the room, and the rug. That useful rug that had brought her and Fitzwilliam together. At this time Georgiana asked at last the question which Elizabeth perceived had been in her mind since long before they had met:

"The Proposal! How did Fitzwilliam propose!" Georgiana's bright eyes lit with the question. "Fitzwilliam tells me nothing." She smiled. "He may be the most attentive of brothers but he does not realize the way that women are desperate for such details. So tell. Tell. Tell. What happened?"

Elizabeth smiled at her softly. "Do you not respect your brother's privacy?"

The girl blushed and looked down, completely extinguished. "Oh. It's wrong to ask? I had thought..."

"No. No. No. It is quite right to ask. A good question but the details..."

Elizabeth hesitated.

Darcy had never even asked. Never asked at all. She had just been told by Mrs. Bennet and Mr. Bennet and then by Mr. Darcy himself that they were to marry. And she had not argued because she had no choice. Never any choice. She was now happy with him, but she still wanted a choice.

She wanted to be asked.

Georgiana blushed and her eyes widened. "Was there something indiscreet?" She then covered her mouth and squeaked. "No. Not Fitzwilliam. He is too proper for anything like that. But, then..."

Too proper for anything like *that*. Ha. Georgiana had *not* taken the true measure of her brother in her hero worship.

Elizabeth laughed tinnily. "To own the truth, it is hard to remember the details. The night was entirely a blur, and it seemed very much as if one moment we were talking about a matter entirely disconnected, and the next…" Elizabeth shrugged and smilingly added, "The next everyone was congratulating me on our plans to marry. I hardly remember how it went between."

"Oh." The tall girl smiled dreamily. "Such a romantic, sweet tale. I want to someday marry someone. Someone who loves me as much as Fitzwilliam loves you. And someone who will make me so perfectly happy and who I can make happy."

Elizabeth smiled at the girl and took her hand, "Georgie — we are to be sisters so you must call me Lizzy — you will. I promise you will. And your proposal will be far more romantic."

"No! Fitzwilliam is too good. And I am… not entirely good."

"You are." Elizabeth lowered her voice and said intently, "I have heard the story, of your… escape."

She startled and looked at Elizabeth with wide eyes. "You have."

"I despise that man. More for what he did to you than for anything else."

"He was not… I was such a silly duckling. No brains in the head. I wouldn't have—"

"Nonsense."

Georgiana sighed.

"Nonsense I say, you were unsupervised, and you were good hearted, and he attempted to use you, and now you are wiser. Fifteen is very young. So is sixteen. You shall grow even wiser yet. I urge you to adopt my philosophy, and look back on the past only as it gives you pleasure."

"Do you really believe that?" The soft voice of the girl was hard to hear.

Elizabeth smiled firmly at her and squeezed her hand. "I believe it firmly."

Georgiana shyly looked up at her from under her eyelashes, and though she still was something of a silly duckling, Elizabeth decided that having Georgie as another sister would be another decided benefit of marrying Mr. Darcy.

Even if he had never asked her.

She wished he had asked her.

Chapter Eleven

There were loud exclamations and dancing, and the sounds of the party through the doorway, but inevitably Elizabeth and Darcy found themselves back, on this night before they were to marry, in the library of Netherfield.

It had been decided that as Bingley and Darcy were the best of friends, and Elizabeth and Jane were the best of sisters, that they would marry together. So tomorrow they were to marry, and Bingley was throwing a grand ball for the entire neighborhood the night before, to celebrate the wedding, but then they would break up early, by ball terms, and be prepared to all march out to the Longbourn chapel the following morn, not a great deal past noon and tie the knot in a double marriage.

Elizabeth and Darcy had danced, and smiled, and talked.

But now they wanted some privacy for a few final kisses before all future kisses would be married kisses.

By mutual agreement the two went to the library, which had several sets of candles set on the tables. They stood side by side admiring the fine, declawed, toothless bear rug.

"I shall persuade the owner, since Bingley insists it is not his place to determine what to do with the piece, to sell it to me."

"And place it in your famed library in Pemberley?"

Darcy grimaced and literally recoiled from the idea.

"I cannot understand," she said as she admired the way the candlelight flickered on his face, "how this could not fit with *every* decorative scheme."

She could barely see it in the low light, but Elizabeth knew Darcy made his skeptical eyebrow raise.

With a laugh, Elizabeth then said, "Our bedroom in that case?"

"Ours," he replied in a low voice, taking her hands in his, and looking meaningfully towards her lips. "You are determined for us to share a bedroom?"

"No," she laughed lightly, "only a bed."

"Ah! But all of the beds in Pemberley are in rooms."

"You have not considered making a bed hallway?"

"A hallway is still a room."

"No it isn't." Elizabeth grinned and bit her lip in that way which usually made him kiss her. He obliged her once again.

Excellent and obliging gentleman that he was.

Thankfully this time Mrs. Bennet did not make an entrance as Darcy carefully buried one hand in her hair, and pulled her tightly against his finely shaped body with the other.

She, rather less carefully, mangled the work of his valet on his hair.

The two slowed and grinned at each other still holding their bodies tight together. Despite the warmth from the glowing coals in the big fireplace, the room was slightly chilled, but neither of them needed any help from something so mundane as *heat* to stay *warm* tonight.

"Tomorrow." Darcy brought his soft lips to her ear, and his warm breath made her shiver. He whispered, "After tomorrow I won't stop myself when I want to kiss you." He kissed her ear. "Nibble you." He nibbled on her ear. "Lick you." He licked her ear.

Helplessly Elizabeth moaned.

Part of her rather wished he would not stop *tonight*. That bear rug would be a fitting object to lose her maidenhead upon. She shuddered closer to him, and gripped his arms and his back.

Darcy groaned and let out a long breath. His eyes were wild, and his hair was delightfully tousled from its even arrangement by her hands. "Tomorrow," he whispered to himself. "Tomorrow."

Elizabeth grinned. "You had those kinds of plans for tomorrow? I myself planned to go to a church, and participate in a religious sacrament."

"You did, were you?"

He looked as if he wanted to grab and kiss her again.

"Yes. You might come with me."

"I might. We could meet in the front of the church."

"Yes, in front of all our friends and family."

The two smiled at each other.

Elizabeth wanted to tell him. She needed to tell him that she loved him. She was marrying him... not out of requirement. But because she wanted to marry him. His eyes, his lips, his hands. The way he spoke to her, the kindness he showed her.

He must love her too.

Darcy took her hand and kissed it. "What are you thinking, my dear?"

"My dear?" Elizabeth swallowed. "You make it sound like we are an old married couple like my parents and..."

"No, what are you thinking?"

She held his hand against her cheek. "I... I love you. Desperately, deeply. I've come to ardently admire you, and longingly love you, and I want *you*. Only you. When I see you happy... I would have chosen to marry you if I could. Even if nothing pushed us together, but just because I want to be your companion for life."

Darcy's face lost its animation. He did not say anything for a moment.

Elizabeth had expected a different reaction to this confession of affection. "Say something, what... what are *you* thinking?"

"Lizzy..." he kissed her hand. "I am glad you are happy. Very, very glad. And—"

"What do you not want to say?" Suddenly Elizabeth had an aching anxiety in her chest. He would not meet her eyes. He was not saying that he loved her. She wanted to hear it. Before they married, she wanted to be told he loved her. "You do love me — you can't... you can't kiss me, and be so sweet, and — it is more than a simple desire for my body, the passion — you must love me."

"I do." He sighed and relaxed, as whatever tension was in him partially went away. He smiled at her, in a way that only half reached his eyes. "I do love you, Elizabeth. I ardently admire and love you."

He grinned, suddenly happy again. "I ardently admire and love you. I have not said so much even to myself before now. But I do. Elizabeth Bennet, I ardently admire and love you."

He pulled her close, and they kissed again. The fear, the weird fear Elizabeth had felt for a moment fled. She enjoyed the taste of his lips, the touch of his hands, the feel of him.

And when they stopped kissing Elizabeth happily smiled into Fitzwilliam Darcy's face. "I am so happy. And you too. I am glad that you are happy."

He did not respond. His face assumed the public mask again.

"You are happy?"

She meant to make it a statement. But it was a question.

Darcy said nothing. He looked from the windows, to the fire, to the candles. His hands on her back gripped her tightly against him. And then he sighed and relaxed his grip. "You cannot — Lizzy, I love you. There is no one else who I would wish more as the companion of my life. I—"

"But you would not marry me. You are not happy."

"What has *happiness* to do with the matter? We are not born to pursue happiness, but duty, and the position of our family, and — happiness is *not* a matter of such import that a great man will submerge his other interests in its pursuit."

"You don't even care about happiness, but you are not happy."

"I would never have chosen this marriage. To marry you is contrary to my judgement, my normal habits of character, and the interests of my family. You *know* that already. It is a simple matter for you to see our marriage as an unalloyed good, for it is solely to your advantage and to the advantage of your family, but I do not pursue *happiness*, or passions, or admiration or love. I have never allowed myself to be moved purely by such considerations before."

Elizabeth felt a terrible pain in her chest. "Do you not — your family has liked me, I think the earl approves of me, and Georgie—"

"He has *no* choice. Just as I have *no* choice. Do not ask me to say I would have chosen this if I had a choice."

"You love me." Elizabeth couldn't breathe quite right. "You would wish to marry me on that account."

"If it was not for that *accident* which led to my passion overcoming my sense for a minute, we never would have married. I would have left Hertfordshire, and schooled myself into good sense and resistance to your charms, and your perfection and your—"

"Don't! No sweet words. Not ever. Not in that tone."

How had this night become a sudden disaster? He even loved her. But not really. If he really loved her he would want to marry her. He would *choose* her if he loved her. And now he was going to be forced into a marriage he despised, and soon he would come to despise her. She could not do it. She could not marry him if he did not wish the marriage. She loved him too much.

"Please... please. We have passed so much together. We have... spoken. Please consider. In your heart, if you were free — suppose you were free—"

"I am not free. Such speculation is useless."

"If you were free, if at this moment there was no tie of social expectation and past choices between us, if your honor did not bind you to marry me — you would not walk away then. Right? You would still, after all we have spoken together. All we have loved together. Our kisses. You would ask me to marry you, would you not? If you were free. Would not the bonds of affection betwixt you and me be enough? Would you marry me? Just tell me."

"No."

One syllable.

One syllable should not be able to tear her heart apart like a knife.

She realized her breath was beginning to hitch desperately, and he would *see* how much she was hurt if she did not say something to hide it. "Is that *all* you have to say for yourself?"

"What do you expect me to say to such a question? Do you wish me to lie? I have told you, my happiness is of less importance than my honor. Than my family."

"Fitzwilliam. I... I wish..."

"In domestic matters we shall be happy. I believe that. Do not doubt that. You are an exceedingly excellent woman. Your mind, your manners, and your sharpness are exactly what I want in a wife. I would pick you *for yourself* if that was all that was at question. Yet, I will not now pretend. I cannot now pretend. My honesty compels me to not now pretend: My good judgement would rebel against the offer. If I were truly free. Your charms are not enough to overcome the deficiencies of your connections, the duty I have to the Darcy name, and the duty I have to my relations."

Just breathe. Breathe evenly. One breath after another.

A pressure crushed her chest. But Elizabeth would have made a fantastic actress.

Elizabeth simply nodded. Tears simply snuck around the edges of her eyes. She let Darcy brush her tears away, as was his wont, without either flinging him away or eating his face with desperate kisses that he would not have chosen if he were free to choose.

She didn't even understand her pain. They were still going to marry.

She wasn't losing anything.

"Lizzy, don't be unhappy. Things are what we make of them. Neither of us have any choice in this matter, and we have chosen to be happy, and that is wise of us and—"

"Don't touch me."

He flinched away from her and paled.

Elizabeth's breath hitched up.

Once. Twice. Sobbing breaths.

She struggled to control herself. "Please," she said quietly. "Let me be at peace. Everything you say. I understand your *character*. Your honesty. Noth— nothing to a-a-apologize for. B-b-but." She was losing her pretence of calm. In a single breath Elizabeth hitched out, "I thought you would answer differently. So kind. You've been so kind."

She panted.

The candles flickered menacingly. Darcy's face was pale with worry. He said, "Don't cry. Please don't cry. I *am* happy you shall be my wife, and—" He looked at her, flexing his hands helplessly. His shoulders stooped in an unwonted, guilty way.

"No lies." Elizabeth's voice was screechy, high pitched. She could barely recognize the sound. She felt as though she were half detached from her body. There was a rushing in her ears. She feared she might faint. "No softenings. You don't want to marry me. Don't change the honesty. Who you are. Who you are. No. No. No change."

He reached out to embrace her and pull her towards him, like he had comforted her before when she cried. Elizabeth jerkily hopped back, staying out of his reach. She shook her head desperately. "I n-n-need. Goodbye, Fitzwilliam. I must alone."

"Lizzy, this is no way to act. We won't see each other again till we marry. I don't want us to part in this way."

She shook her head. Side to side. She stumbled back against the door.

He came to her. She hurled the door open, and she rushed out of the room, into the hallway.

The library. That fateful room which had brought them together.

It would be always a hateful sight. Elizabeth swore to herself that once Jane had married Bingley, she would never enter that doorway again.

She hurried down the hall, knowing Darcy might come after her.

Why did this hurt so much? She couldn't have expected he would *choose* her, how had she been such an featherwit?

Elizabeth was shivering when she reached the stables. Their coach driver played cards with his counterparts from the other families at the party.

"Miss Elizabeth." The old servant stood up worriedly when he saw her stand at the entrance to the little heated room next to the kitchen where the servants sat. She knew she must be a sight, with tears down her face and a trembling stomach.

"John, I need... need. Home. I need, must return. Now, at once. Apologies, but you... you will need to return for the family after."

A single careful look over her and he nodded.

Soon safe in the carriage, trundling home with the lamps swinging side to side lighting the grey leafless hedges and trees.

They clattered past cold houses with high pointed roofs and lit candles thinly burning through the windows.

*****

Darcy had not known what to do when Elizabeth fled. His first instinct had been to hunt her down. But he did not know what to say.

He had never seen Elizabeth like that.

So instead of following her he walked to the window of the library and looked down the unlit road outside. Even with his excellent eyes he could see almost nothing in such a dark. There was a slight reflection of his from the candlelight in the window. He did not like the look of his own face and neatly tied cravat at this moment, and he turned away, staring at the ceiling.

How had the night gone so wrong?

He ground his jaw together.

What did the woman expect?

He promised to care for her. He brought his uncle to witness the ceremony, and browbeat him until he agreed to support them both in society. He told her they would be happy. He had determined to be happy. He had brought her gifts, and he was giving her his name.

What did Elizabeth expect?

What was the use of a *bloody* useless question?

Would he marry her if he had the choice?

They had *no* choice. He never had a choice. Ever since that moment she fell into his arms, with those wide eyes, and he felt her body in his arms. And then her mother interrupted them.

No choice. Not for him. Not for her. They had to marry, so why *ask* if he would choose the marriage.

Damnation.

His life was as controlled as hers — more so. He lost in the marrying, she gained. Even though Elizabeth had not tried to trap him into this, she gained from the marriage. And they loved each other, so what she had wished, even that would be fulfilled.

She had nothing to complain about.

He would be a good husband. He *had* been a good affianced partner during the course of their period of courtship.

He would care for her, and adore her, and love her, and kiss her, and show her respect, and never violate their vows, and bring her to live in one of the greatest estates in England, connect her to families far above her own, shower her with pin money and other chances for expenditure, caress her when she needed caressing, comfort her when she needed comforting, and support her when she needed supporting. Despite their many deficiencies, he would aid her family as if they were his own, and never again speak a word against their characters.

The sound of the carriage clattering off made him look through the window again. With hanging lanterns swinging side to side was the now familiar Longbourn carriage rocking slightly as it trundled down the road.

She was leaving him and not coming back.

The back of the wooden chair Darcy gripped cracked with a startling and loud shatter, like a small gunshot in the dark room.

What did the damned woman want?

*****

She wanted a choice.

Darcy wanted a choice.

And Darcy had *made* his choice clear.

His choice was not her, and she would respect that choice.

Elizabeth gasped with pain as she sat, forehead against the cold window, in her dark room.

A man liking money and connections and *honor* more than her. Darcy's choice should not hurt. There was no rational sense here. No reason for this hurt so much. No *sense*. *Stop* hurting.

Elizabeth sat back at the delicate lady's desk in her room, with a pot of ink and sheets of paper to write on. The slender moon poked through the window, providing little light. A single guttering candle sat, wax tears slowly falling towards the cup on her deck.

She was not going to marry Mr. Darcy. That had been decided by her even before she escaped the room.

Her hands shook and when she picked up a quill to write an explanation to Jane, and through Jane to the rest of her family, of what she was doing, she'd snapped the pen.

She couldn't face him tomorrow and tell him that they were not going to marry.

She also could not face her mother's screams, her sister's worries, the fear that something would go wrong between Jane and Bingley after she refused Darcy.

But mainly she could not face *him*.

He would tell her that she was engaged in dramatics. He would tell her that they had to marry, that they would find domestic happiness. He would tell her to just go to the church with him. And she would not be able to stop herself from following where he led, not when he was leading her to marriage with him. She would be able to pretend, for a few hours, that it was what he truly wanted — then too late.

The air was still and firm with cold.

Even in her bedroom, despite the banked fire whose coals glowed dimly the air made her hands to numb and her leg hairs to prickle upwards in goose bumps.

Elizabeth did not trust herself to stand firm to what she knew was right.

There would be so much noise.

She would have to say no to Darcy again and again as he said they should marry. He would *not* accept the extra scandal of a broken engagement easily.

She had to go somewhere that they could not importune her endlessly.

Elizabeth knew that was not the real reason she wanted to disappear. She could say no, if she really needed to. And she could keep to her resolution, knowing it was the right resolution.

No, she wanted to leave because she felt like a wounded animal which needed to find a cave to hide in until she either bled out from the injury or recovered.

She would give Darcy his choice, and she would choose her own future. A blank dead future. A winter future. But after winter came spring. After years of time, she would no longer hurt so much, and be once again able to fall in love with a different man, a man who would choose her.

No. No. She didn't want to fall in love with another man. No. The possibility was worse, more terrible, than being alone forever. Forgetting Darcy.

Why. Why. Why. Why. Why.

Elizabeth closed her eyes again, and rehearsed her plan.

Pack a neat light valise. She had a large heavy bag stored in her closet which she could get without making any great noise. A single spare dress and some underclothing. Cold outside, so she needed to wear several petticoats. She felt gloomily certain that tomorrow would be a day when the frost would not melt even in the afternoon sun, and the icy smells of winter would infuse everything. It would be a day when young women should stay at home about their fires, enjoying the popping pine smell, and the taste of melted chocolate and the fragrances of hot tea or toddy.

Maybe Papa would never forgive her for this further impropriety, running away from her own wedding. Maybe she would never be able to see her room, or even her sisters, again.

Jane would surely understand, and she and Bingley — what if Bingley refused to marry Jane after she jilted Darcy?

No. You cannot think that.

She was giving Darcy what he wanted, and he would understand, and explain to Bingley why he must still marry Jane. She would beg him to do that, upon his honor, in her letter to him.

Five miles walk, not to the coach station in Meryton, but the one the next village over. It would take her two hours, but exercise should keep her warm enough to not freeze even in this weather. She would bundle in a thick puffy fur lined coat and wear a half dozen petticoats under and wrap her chest in three chemises. The morning post going north would pass through there about an hour after she arrived at the station, and she would take it north.

No need for a corset. Also she would have no one to help her put it on. Nice, freeing, to not be bound by the stiff whalebone. Her choice.

The house was quiet enough that Elizabeth was no longer scared of discovery. She dressed and packed by the light of the flickering wax candle.

Once she was fully dressed, Elizabeth sat down at her lady's desk, made of fine yellow woods, and embroidered with Chinese floral patterns.

She stared at the paper. Her hands trembled again.

Two letters were needed. She could write in one to Jane everything Papa must hear.

That was not the letter which hurt.

The letter which hurt was the one to Darcy.

Tired. Cold. She didn't want to start the walk. It seemed like a terrible painful prospect she knew she must take on.

The candles flickered hypnotically. Their reflection glinted off her dark window. Outside, she saw the crescent moon which was well started on its slow descent towards the dawn. Her room was suddenly and unspeakably dear to her.

Her intent was to hide away time enough for the scandal to dissipate and then return once her husbanded funds exhausted themselves, and she wrote as much to Jane.

She had fifteen pounds put away, which was more than enough for a month or two to be spent comfortably in a boarding house in some distant market town. And for her to then be able to return and face her final fate.

Maybe Papa would be so angry he would not let her return.

Elizabeth shivered. She did not think that was in Papa's nature, but many fathers would respond so to a girl who was acting as she was. Maybe she would never see her comfortable girlish room again, just as she would never see the inside of the mistress's apartments in Pemberley.

And now she had been staring at the candles, at the window, and at her own fears for fifteen minutes without writing a word.

Elizabeth decisively dipped the quill into the ink pot, and wrote her letters. The letter to Jane was easy, full of logistics, sweet goodbyes, and promises of seeing one another again in a few months. She told Jane that she wanted her to marry Bingley anyways tomorrow, even without her there.

The letter to Mr. Darcy was hard to write. But Elizabeth did, quickly, and decisively and in the course of less than an hour.

And then there was no more time to delay if she wished to be out of the neighborhood before dawn.

Packed and prepared, Elizabeth Bennet set out into the clear icy night, lit by the waning crescent of a half moon and the spangled rich banner of stars prickling the heavens like the tears which prickled her eyes and froze onto her cheeks, and silent except for the crunch of the icy dirt beneath her boots and the sniffles she could not stop, as she walked away from her life, her marriage, and the man she knew more than ever before that she loved.

Chapter Twelve

The sharp razor wielded by Darcy's valet scraped again and again across his cheeks to give him a clean, close shave, preparing him to look his finest for his wedding.

He should have chased after Elizabeth and done something to comfort her... was it even true? She had no right to expect him to claim that he would have offered to marry her without any compulsion, but... though it *would* have been against his best judgement, and his normal habits of character, and contrary to the interests of his family, the longer Darcy thought upon it, the less he cared.

It would have been the wrong choice, but he would have offered to marry her, because he loved her so ardently, had it been his choice.

Why couldn't he have told her *that* yesterday night?

He needed to see Elizabeth. He needed to tell her. Darcy didn't want her to be weeping and unhappy as they said their vows.

The wedding parties planned to meet at Longbourn and then walk to Elizabeth's parish church together. He could ask to take her aside and speak to her then. They were to reach the house at ten, so there would be ample time for him to comfort her before the time when they could marry passed at noon.

But would he make her happy? She did not only desire him to say he would marry her, overcome by passion and affection that he could not control, and against his better judgement if he had the choice. She wanted him to say that she was his unalloyed choice, and that every other consideration was of far less moment next to her happiness.

Well he certainly wanted to marry her.

The scent of the richly lathered shaving soap filled Darcy's dressing room, along with anxiety for Elizabeth. She had been so... struck the previous night.

He should not have just let her walk away, and then run away like that.

She had been trembling.

But why?

Women were generally overly sensitive and irrational creatures. But he had never detected any of that sort of frailty in Elizabeth before. She could be driven by her passions and temper, but Darcy had learned he could be as well. It would be the rankest hypocrisy to criticise her for that, so Darcy did not.

She could not have expected him to say he *rationally* wanted to marry her. She had been so... distraught. He didn't want his Elizabeth to ever be worried or sad. He didn't want her to be anxious, or frantic, or whatever that emotion she had shown yesterday evening was.

While his valet used the leather strop to resharpen his blade before switching to Darcy's right cheek, Darcy felt sick inside. He was tired, and he hoped his eyes did not show it. He had not been able to sleep for half the night as Elizabeth's pale worried visage stayed before his eyes.

It was worse than any feeling he'd known since his father died. To know Elizabeth hurt, and that her hurt was his fault.

She had looked so sad.

He wanted to hug her. And comfort her. And hold her close, and kiss her till she was senseless, and then kiss her again, once she was already senseless from his kisses. But she had refused to let him.

He loved her.

The soft feel of the towel patting off his face. The valet frowned and critically examined his work, before he nodded to Darcy. "Good enough for marrying. Good enough, if I say so myself. And congratulations, sir."

Darcy nodded his head and smiled acceptance.

He *loved* her.

Even though he'd hurt her, he would make it up to her, and never let her hurt again. Somehow he would make her happy and smiling again. Smiling at him. And tonight they would be together, alone, him and her, with nothing between them. One flesh.

Darcy stood from the chair and removed his bathrobe. He quickly with the help of the valet shifted into the fine suit he had ordered specially from London for his wedding day and only worn for fitting so far. It clung to his undergarments and his body like a glove. Darcy examined himself in the mirror for a long minute.

He would look satisfactory at the church, even standing next to such a beauty as Elizabeth.

He held out his hand and a fine white silk cloth was handed to him by the valet, and he did the work to tie and shape his cravat on his own. He was no Beau Brummel, and often paid little attention to the intricacies of his personal appearance, but on this day he ought to look his best for Elizabeth.

Fully dressed, Darcy descended the stairs to the breakfast room to grab a quick bite to settle his stomach before they rode out to Longbourn. His uncle was still at his bath, Colonel Fitzwilliam and Bingley stood about. Bingley nervously examined himself in a mirror. He wheeled on Darcy. "You are sure Jane will not run away at the last minute? I cannot be so lucky. I cannot."

Darcy smiled at his friend and placed his hand on Bingley's shoulder. "You are so lucky."

Colonel Fitzwilliam laughed. "Not due to your good advice — remember this lesson, Bingley: never listen overmuch to our excessively vertical friend."

There was a sound of a single horse coming up the road and stopping in front of the house. Then a fierce knocking on the door. Darcy felt a tight anxiety. As if this meant something was wrong with Elizabeth.

Bingley said, "I hope this is not Mr. Bennet come to say that Jane has changed her mind and shall not marry me."

The gentleman was in fact Mr. Bennet. He burst into the breakfast room with a storm cloud upon his face. Bingley blanched.

"You drove my daughter off. You… you… damn you to a dark hell."

Bingley waved his hands. "I didn't mean to do anything!"

"Not you! *That* damned damnable disagreeable devil."

Darcy's face whitened. "Elizabeth! Where is she?"

"Where? Where? The deuce. You *now* care about her wellbeing. Somewhere between here and the hell you come from. I hope she does not return until I am well and finally finished with *you*."

Colonel Fitzwilliam said in his amiable manner, "Intelligence man, intelligence. Can't make heads or tails of this — Miss Elizabeth ran off you say. Can't imagine why a woman might ever want to jilt Darcy."

"Damn you. You rich, careless gentlemen. Damn you all. Not joke."

"Calm down, if Miss Elizabeth is in any danger, we will aid you in finding her, but calm yourself."

"Calm! Calm! This man." Mr. Bennet angrily stabbed his finger in Darcy's face. "Kissed. Kissed *my* daughter. No permission. No asking. No concern for honor, either hers or his. And *now* he has driven my daughter away."

"I did not. I did nothing to—"

"Damn you." Mr. Bennet hissed at Darcy. He pulled a folded page from his coat pocket. "A letter, from my daughter to you."

He shoved it into Darcy's face, the residue of the red wax that had sealed it stuck like driplets of blood to the creamy, almost yellow, paper.

"You read my correspondence?" Darcy said, rather offended, as he took the smooth heavy paper into his hand, and opened it to read.

"By Jove. You damned, you damned — may God bloody bleed you." Mr. Bennet's eyes apoplectically bugged out from his face. "My daughter disappeared. Having left an only half articulate note to Jane about how she has realized she cannot marry you, and not to worry, because she has a little money so she can disappear for three months, and that she would be back eventually. Of course I read the *damned* letter she wrote to you."

Colonel Fitzwilliam poured three thick tumblers of whisky as Mr. Bennet ranted, and he stuffed one into Mr. Bennet's hand the moment the older man paused to take a breath. "Bad form, reading another gentleman's correspondence. But that's a full cannon shot worth of good excuse for it."

Mr. Bennet glared at Colonel Fitzwilliam, clearly unappeased by the approval of Darcy's cousin for his violating Darcy's mail. Even if he *did* have a legitimate excuse for doing so. Colonel Fitzwilliam grinned insouciantly, and stretched his muscular arms behind his head.

"Now," Mr. Bennet turned back to Mr. Darcy, and warmed to his subject once again, "I only have to regret that I ever was so stupid, so craven, and so criminally negligent as a parent as to give my permission and blessing to a match I *knew* was ill advised and ill placed to lead to happiness on the part of either party. You brute. You ungentlemanly, damnable, unchristian brute — by Jove. By Jove, I have no pride in how I treat my wife. But I at the least show her more affection and trust than you do — and to Lizzy, who deserves every form of consideration. And after you two had spent so much time with one another, and I had thought — damn you. But you ought to know — even if Lizzy is found, I withdraw *my* permission for the match. I'll not have you near. Not have you near my daughter ever again. So read the damned letter — or not. I give not a damn."

Mr. Bennet then left the room, followed by Bingley who pestered him, "Jane — how is Jane. Of course we cannot marry today, not with Lizzy missing, but do I still have your permission. For Jane?"

"The *deuce*! I hold you in great blame for bringing that disgraceful creature into my neighborhood, but Jane would be heartbroken if I tossed *you* away. Marry her whenever you want. Today still. I care not. *You* remaining a bachelor will do nothing to find my Lizzy."

Bennet opened the front door and an instant later slammed it shut.

Bingley slunk back into the breakfast room as Darcy read Elizabeth's letter:

Mr. Darcy, you have made it exceedingly clear, in every way, that you do not wish to marry me.

I love you. Desperately. You, through being yourself have brought me to love you, but though you claim to love me, I know you do not, not in truth.

No.

That is not fair.

You do love me. But you love other considerations more. Your honor. Your family. Your position in society.

I was so... I have been such a fool. A goose. A silly duckling, like your dear sister calls herself. An irrational, senseless, foolish, naïve, in a word, a girl.

I have been a passionate, foolish girl.

I thought I was above this — I truly believed you would tell me you would choose me. I have felt, during the course of our engagement, as though I had no choice. I wanted to have that choice. If I told you that you were my choice, and then you replied that now that we knew each other. If you had replied that now that we had mingled our souls you wished us to marry, then I would have been happy and satisfied.

My soul is mingled with yours, even though yours cannot be mingled with mine, for if you had truly mingled your soul with mine, you never would have been able to reject me. Your judgement and your character and your nature would then rebel against refusing me as surely as it would rebel against cutting off your own hand.

I grow lachrymose. I am tearful and foolish, and I speak irrationally again: Of course you would choose what is best for your position and your family. You would not engage in girlish fantasies drawn from a novel.

I should never have expected you to say anything different than what you did say. But I did expect you to choose me.

And now I know what your choice is. And now I know that you do not choose me.

I… I love you. And now I know that for that reason I cannot marry you.

I am going to leave for a while. There shall be a scandal, and you shall not like to see your name mixed up with it, but the blame in matters of honor will entirely go to me. It will be impossible for you to marry me, and thus you will feel no guilt, no loss of honor in not marrying me.

This is my choice, finally I have a choice, and I choose to release you.

I beg you, please, as you love me, and as you know you owe me some debt in honor for that first kiss — please encourage Bingley to marry my sister. I fear that the scandal or your displeasure with me, or some manner of that sort will break matters between them up, and leave my sister heartbroken, my family's fortunes adrift in the sequence to the scandal, and me with a permanent additional guilt for seeking to ensure your happiness at the cost of theirs.

So please, as I give you back your choice, and let you have what you wished in the matter of our marriage, please ensure, for me, that Bingley and Jane fulfill their choice.

The memory of our kisses, of our embraces, of those sweet interludes shall always be precious. I swear to never forget you. You are the first man that I have loved, and I only wished you could have chosen to desire me at your side as the companion of your life. But to force a marriage you do not wish upon you, would be the most terrible fate I could imagine for myself.

So goodbye, Mr. Darcy, goodbye. And may God bless you,

Yours,

E Bennet

Long breaths. Darcy breathed deeply trying to calm.

Darcy desperately stared at the letter. He hoped to see some clue to where she was in it.

The paper was speckled with water marks and blurred ink from her tears.

But no hint as to where she had gone.

"Report, what is the information from the letter?" Colonel Fitzwilliam sharply demanded.

"She is gone. I drove her away. I told her last night that I would not have chosen to marry her if we were not forced to by being observed during a kiss. She believed me and has fled so I will not need to marry her."

"Ah." Colonel Fitzwilliam's face cleared, and he poured himself a new shot of whiskey as Darcy spoke. "And we know from Mr. Bennet's report that she has sufficient money to remain afield for several months. Matters seem in good course. I foresee that you will not marry today."

Colonel Fitzwilliam pushed the decanter towards Bingley who tilted his head to the side and shrugged before pouring himself a tumbler.

"In good course!" Darcy almost shrieked at Colonel Fitzwilliam.

The officer phlegmatically shrugged and sipped his whiskey.

His cousin was being an ass.

He needed to think: where would Elizabeth go? Darcy closed his eyes. At least he had Colonel Fitzwilliam's help, but that was no guarantee that he could find her. He had seen how Wickham hid from his cousin in London. But Wickham had been an experienced and skilled sewer rat. Elizabeth was a young gentlewoman, with no experience hiding herself, between him and Colonel Fitzwilliam they could find her.

A private detective?

No, at least not at first. Elizabeth would not wish to be found and bothered by such a man, and one would not be able to hold her in place until Darcy found her and... and — What would he do when he found Elizabeth?

Tell her that he wanted to marry her.

Beg her until she understood that was his true wish.

"I need your help. Both of you. You must help me! We must find her immediately."

Colonel Fitzwilliam had picked up the day's newspaper and flapped the pages open to read and he had finished his whiskey and replaced it with a pot of coffee he'd ordered from the kitchen whose rich aroma filled the room. Colonel Fitzwilliam stilled in the middle of bringing his cup to his lips. He put the mug down on Bingley's lacquered breakfast table. "By Athena's wise owls, why?"

"This is a matter of *import*, not a time for your nonsense Grecian deity oaths!"

"I repeat my question: By Athena's *wise* owls, why?"

"For God's sake, *she* is missing."

"You mean the fortune hunter? I should think *you* would be pleased to be rid of her. Quite strange for a fortune hunter—"

"Damnation! Richard. You make me want to throttle you."

"Hahahahaha. I like to see some spirit in you! Too reserved for my taste in the usual course of things. But ha! Elizabeth is doing you good."

"I can go up north, along the roads, and check at any inns there, and question for her presence, while you go to London, and—"

"Darcy, there is absolutely no reason for me to search for Elizabeth."

"She is *missing*."

"Did you read her letter? Because I am thinking you did not, despite reporting on its contents to me."

"What are you talking about?"

"Miss Elizabeth is in the precise location where she chooses to be. Wherever that is. Without us. I am quite satisfied that if she needs any help, she knows where to find it. A clever, capable and sensible gentlewoman, who had some money with her. I worry more by far about that big brown horse of yours throwing you, and you cracking your hard head open while you gallopingly gallivant desperately looking for the lady than I do for *her* health."

"I must find her. I must. I must tell her that—"

"You must sit down and have a drink, and think upon your own failings."

Darcy paced restlessly.

"It is quite clear from what she wrote what will happen." Colonel Fitzwilliam calmly sipped his coffee as he spoke. "She will remain in her mysterious location long enough that she is sure you no longer feel an obligation to marry her. Then she will return to Meryton. And then you must court her properly. I hope for your sake she doesn't encounter an even more fetching young man whilst hiding in the wilds. But, though I very much hope she *will* be my cousin still, the whole experience would still be good for you, even if Miss Elizabeth jilts you in final truth."

Looked at that way Darcy could see why his cousin could phlegmatically stay in Netherfield instead of hunting down the roads for Elizabeth.

It even made *Darcy* feel a little better, to think that he probably didn't need to worry about her being dead in some ditch, or starving while wandering the moors like a Yorkshire governess run off to avoid ravishment by her employer.

Colonel Fitzwilliam looked up from the newspaper again. "By the by, I'd hire a spy in Meryton, if I were you, to give you accurate intelligence of when Elizabeth returns. Wouldn't be surprised if Bennet wrings a promise out of Bingley to tell you nothing. Any case, I've had letters from Bingley. Best have some news from someone *legible*, eh?"

"Hey!" Bingley exclaimed. "I am still here." He shrugged. "I agree. No need to be scared about Lizzy. She'll shift well enough."

Colonel Fitzwilliam stood and cradled the saucer of his coffee cup in his left hand. "Darcy, need to confess — you sounded like an idiot when you first told me about Elizabeth. Left me *quite* worried."

"What are you talking about?"

"The very fact that you would marry a lady who you believed to have intrigued to entrap you, under any circumstances, it made no sense to me. Only when I saw you two together did I realize at last that you, the Great Fitzwilliam Darcy, with your many virtues and annoying habit of overlooking matters obvious to others had overlooked your own capacity for self-deception."

"Self-deception!"

"What passion you have though — still waters *do* run deep — *I* always knew you had it in you. Everyone else called you a wet blanket, a stick in the mud, a... well anyway, kissing a girl in Bingley's library during a ball! You showed *them*. And excellent move, catching her when she *tripped*, you should be shamed, by—"

"I get your point," Darcy sourly snapped back. He'd just been *jilted* by the woman he adored, after telling her, among other things, that he ardently admired her, and his cousin could think of no better way to help him than to make fun of him.

"Bingley," Colonel Fitzwilliam looked at the grinning man. "It was quite wrong of him to impose on your hospitality in that way to ravish mouthily a guest of yours."

"Not in the slightest," Bingley replied laughingly. "I am quite happy due to the consequent. Do you know, Caroline confessed to me that she had a scheme laid to follow me to London and convince me to abandon Jane? It quite well might have worked — an inability to humbly confess to faults is not one of *my* faults—"

"There are gentlemen here for whom that *is* one of their faults."

Both Bingley and Colonel Fitzwilliam looked at Darcy.

"I know I have failed! This is entirely my doing. Why aren't you more worried, Bingley! She is to be your sister."

"And as my sister, I have the highest opinion in her cleverness, competence, general abilities, and specific abilities. I think very highly of Miss Elizabeth, so I have no worries on *her* account. She is well, I am certain, and when she has decided she has had enough of the game, and time enough has passed, she will return to visibility. No worries *there*. The only question is, will you be ready to properly pursue her?"

"Jilting me the day of my wedding. She was so... so... last night, but I didn't know what to say." Darcy replied, anxiously and absently. He needed to find her. He needed to tell her something. To tell her to stop this silly game and to just *marry him*. He just wanted her to marry him.

He didn't care about anything else.

Bingley grimaced. "I hurt with you, Darcy. If I imagine Jane wrote such a letter to me." He placed a hand upon Darcy's back. "For my part I still hope to marry Jane today, but if you desire me to wait, and —"

"I don't sympathise with him in the *slightest*," Colonel Fitzwilliam said. "And the delectable Jane Bennet — that is a girl who deserves her husband's embrace." Colonel Fitzwilliam winked at Bingley who blushed. "Don't act like a virgin. You know what I mean, and you know how to please a woman. Just remember, she will be your wife. She deserves your detailed attention to her pleasure *more* than a floozy you found in a brothel."

"A floozy! I've never... well, I never..."

Now it was Darcy's turn to raise one eyebrow eye skeptically at Bingley. They had gone to university together. Bingley had been cautious to avoid the pox, but he most certainly *had*.

"Never a floozy found in a brothel!"

"Does that mean," Colonel Fitzwilliam enquired with a salacious wink, "that you found a woman in a brothel who was *not* a floozy, or that you found the floozy on the street, or under a bridge, or in a tavern, but *not* in a brothel — if it was a tavern, perhaps it was also a brothel, and you simply were not aware."

"She *wasn't* a floozy, and it *wasn't* in a brothel!"

"If you insist." Colonel Fitzwilliam spread his hands wide. "You *do* know what you must do when with a woman? Or should I explain, just to be certain? That woman. Your Jane Bennet — she is such a perfect creature that—"

"I would kindly ask you — and I shall not repeat myself — to refrain entirely from commentary upon the figure and charms of my wife." Bingley sounded sharper and more commanding, and more self-assured than Darcy had ever heard him.

"That's my man — but only if you promise to marry her, and to bed her today."

"I am entirely committed upon that project." Bingley glared at Colonel Fitzwilliam, as though the man intended to seduce Jane.

"Good," Colonel Fitzwilliam said decided. "Now let us return to the true idiot of the day. Our villain, Mr. Darcy."

"She jilted me — this is not only my fault."

"Our villain who is making a pretence of being a victim. You *told* her that you did not want to marry her, when a sweet woman asked you if you did. And now you blame *her* for not marrying you to save you from doing what you said you did not want to do?"

"I know I have been a fool." Darcy sighed. "I know this is principally my fault."

"And with *that* confession," Colonel Fitzwilliam said, satisfied, "my day has reached its apogee."

Jane Bennet entered the room. Her hair was pinned back in a simple and quick manner, and she wore a dress that did not have every ruffle and tuck perfectly in place. This did nothing to detract from the serene beauty of the woman.

Behind her bustled Mrs. Bennet. "Heavens! Promise! You must still marry her! Oh! Oh! Oh! My nerves! I am destroyed. I shall never recover! Never!"

"I still shall marry her," Darcy said severely. "Soon as I can find where she has gone, and convince her. I will marry her at the soonest possible chance."

"I was talking to Bingley." Mrs. Bennet blinked at Darcy. "I thought you had jilted Lizzy. Mr. Bennet said that you did not want to marry her anymore. What are you still doing here?"

"I am not such a man as can be changed from my intentions so easily. It would be contrary to my honor to leave your daughter."

"Heavens! Oh! There must be some terrible misunderstanding. For I am quite sure Lizzy thinks you did not want to marry her. I did not understand how she could look so down and sad — she claimed it was only a headache. I knew! A mother's caring affections *always* know when something is amiss with their daughter. She looked so sad and pale. She was trembling. I knew something was wrong, but she needed just to sleep I thought. And then that letter. She thought you jilted her. Oh a terrible misunderstanding! You must still marry her — do say you will—"

"I shall."

"As soon as we find her. Mr. Bennet is doing nothing. Lord! I do not understand my husband. He just came back and he now sits in his study and stares at a decanter of port, without drinking any. I depend on *you*, Mr. Darcy, to find Lizzy. She would only have run away this way if she was convinced you had jilted her. I know her. She is a good girl, who would do everything to make you happy. Oh! You do still want to marry her?"

"I do."

"Then you must go—"

"I am quite sure Miss Elizabeth is well," Colonel Fitzwilliam broke in with an annoyed voice. "And Mr. Darcy will do everything to find her and marry her still. He is not such an idiot as to let this *misunderstanding* stand."

"But, Bingley!" Mrs. Bennet turned to the other gentleman in the room. "Heavens! We will be ruined when Mr. Darcy never finds Lizzy. You must still marry Jane!"

Bingley and Jane had been embracing and whispering softly to each other during the whole of Mrs. Bennet's nervous rant, every word of which pounded deeper into Darcy his sense of having failed Elizabeth.

"What?" Bingley asked with an expression that showed he had no idea what had been said to him.

"You must marry Jane! Today. Before you can change your mind. Heavens! No one cares the slightest for my nerves. Certainly not Mr. Bennet."

"Why wouldn't I marry Jane?"

"Oh." Mrs. Bennet blinked at him. "Of course you want to marry Jane. Look at her! My daughter, she is sweet, and well behaved, and beautiful, and nothing like... of course you want to marry her."

"Jane," Bingley said, "we would not honor your sister's desires if we waited to marry. There is still time to reach the church before noon, and I... I think that well..." Then Bingley exclaimed in his good natured voice, "We should use it. We should marry today!"

"Do you mean that?" Jane's face glowed red with happiness, and a beaming smile that was so pretty it almost hurt Darcy to look upon it. "Even with Lizzy disappearing?"

"My dearest, sweetest, loveliest. My angel. My blonde Jane. Your hair is like gold, and your skin like silk." Jane giggled. "I doubted once. But now that I know *your* affections are mine, *mine* are ever yours. In permanence. Let us marry, immediately, and then your mother will know she has nothing to worry about, no matter how terribly scandalous the scandal becomes."

"Oh, Mr. Bingley!"

The two kissed, softly, sweetly, and with far less passion — though more cute murmurings — than when Darcy and Elizabeth kissed.

Colonel Fitzwilliam pumped his fist in encouragement, silently, as he did not want disrupt the show the two made.

Darcy *knew*, more than at any point before, that he had been an idiot of anti-Napoleonic proportions when he drove Elizabeth to leave.

Jove. He needed to find her. He needed to apologize. And he needed to show her he now understood his failings — he could see them so clearly — and he could become a better man for her sake, a man worthy of a woman worthy of being loved.

Right after he witnessed Bingley's wedding of course.

Chapter Thirteen

While upon the road Elizabeth did not have any expectation of being chased by Darcy, and for that reason she was not worried about pursuit, having a good sense of her father's capabilities and likely response to her disappearance.

This belief that Darcy would not pursue her was a natural expectation given that he did not wish to marry her, and she was doing him a great favor by leaving the day of their marriage.

She hurt in the mind and heart.

Her stomach ached constantly. She felt like a heavy weight pressed on her. Sometimes she could barely pant out her breaths. But she did not cry much. Instead with painfully dry eyes, unblinking, she observed the other passengers in the stage coach as they rushed northward over the course of what was to have been her wedding day.

One town. A pause for ten minutes. On and off. The blacksmith and the customs officer off. An old lady with a tinily printed bible, big spectacles, and a carpet bag on. The old lady tried to talk to Elizabeth, but just as she had been to the two former inhabitants of the coach, she was silent towards the woman, who then subsided, and began to carefully pick through the Bible in the midday sun, her finger dragging along the tiny lines of print.

Elizabeth began to nod off. She was so tired, but there was nowhere to put her head, and the carriage bumped again and again. She could not stay completely miserable in the heart for this long, and she had already suppressed her tears three times.

She hadn't remembered to bring something to read. She had nothing to do.

And she was so sleepy.

Crash and thunk.

The shaking of the carriage shocked Elizabeth awake again. Elizabeth had never been so thoroughly miserable. Yet the combination of physical misery with her mental distress somehow alleviated her. The ringing of the bells on a church they clattered past proclaimed the time to be two o'clock. The coach had turned off the great Northern road, trundling into Northamptonshire by a different way.

Elizabeth neither knew, nor cared, where she was headed.

But at the next stop on the coach's journey she carefully looked about for all her goods — tired as she was, she was too terrified of needing to beg a stranger to send a letter to her father to rescue her immediately because she had left her money in the carriage to make the mistake of leaving any of her bags or supplies behind.

This market town had a sizeable and respectable inn, and she immediately went into it.

During the travel north in the carriage, she had determined upon a name to give herself. Miss E Hayes.

Hayes was a frequent name, but it was *not* Smith. She was quite sure that if there was any pursuit that reached this inn — which she did not expect — the pursuing party would ask for a Smith of her description at every roadside inn. They would of course never think to ask for a Hayes.

Elizabeth signed the register with a blocky script that could not be recognizable as hers, but which might be recognized as the hand of someone awkwardly trying to disguise their cursive.

Once the servant opened the room to her and gave her the keys, Elizabeth sat on the bed, planning to undress as soon as she had energy to do so.

Everything was dark and silent when she woke up.

For a long time Elizabeth stared at the ceiling. She felt sore and terrible. She was still wearing her tightly laced shoes, and she should remove them. Maybe. Maybe she could just stand and leave this inn like she left Longbourn and keep walking into the endless wilderness until she fell into a ditch in the dark, moonless night, and broke her ankle.

The sounds of the nighttime post rolling through the town clattered faintly up. It paused for a few minutes, and then, without as far as Elizabeth could tell, anyone exiting or entering the carriage, the mail set off again.

Silence once more.

The building creaked.

If this was a melodramatic novel, after she walked off into the darkness, and broke her ankle in the ditch, she would nearly starve while stuck at the bottom, hoping desperately to be saved by a passerby. Then, by some ridiculous coincidence, Darcy would find her. He would be completely contrite, and he would beg her for her forgiveness and her hand. He would pick her up from where she had fallen, unable to move, with those muscular arms that had caught her when she tripped, and hugged her many times since then. With those lean fingered hands that she could watch forever, and then he would hold her tight against his chest and kiss her long and sweet.

And then, since this was a melodramatic novel, she would die of her injuries immediately, in his arms.

A long sigh and Elizabeth sat up on the bed and with a thunk that startled her in the night silence — not even insects or mice moved in the middle of winter such as this — she put her feet on the floor and stood. At least she could comfort herself with the fact that she was not in a novel, and that while Darcy was not likely to find her in this remote inn, she was also not likely to be killed by cause of the author wanting the audience to weep.

The room was freezing, and her hands were numb with the cold. Cold in the room seemed to pour from the window, so she walked to the window and looked at the starry spangled sky above.

It was beautiful. The swordsman Orion stood high and proud in the sky, his starry sword belted on his waist, ready for whatever use the sky warrior had waited all the millennia of human history for. Vast and clear, and beautiful.

There were no clear skies like clear December skies. Elizabeth felt a deep full peace, and a connection to the sublime delights of nature.

Then the feeling caught in her chest once more. The agonized tearing.

Darcy saying it, saying he did not wish to marry her.

She hadn't fled to escape the need to marry him. She could have done that by simply not walking downstairs yesterday morning, and by shouting at Mama that she was, once again, her least favorite daughter.

But then Darcy would have come — most likely, it would have been far worse if he hadn't come — and she would have needed to talk to him and see him again.

She had run away from him, not the marriage, from him.

She pulled the rickety wooden chair to the window and put her elbows on the cold wooden sill and cried heartily. But when Elizabeth was done, she got up and went back to bed feeling far better about herself.

The next day she woke early in the morning, breakfasted in the common room, and explained several times the flimsy story she had concocted to explain why she was here alone — a story which none of her listeners fully believed, but they were all too polite to say directly to her face which salacious story they invented for themselves. After a light breakfast she set off for a walk which took her in a giant circuit around this new neighborhood. She stamped and stamped without eating for ten hours, until her feet were exhausted and she was sweaty and hot despite the cold winds blowing through her coat.

She was not at all sure if she could find her way back to the inn and her bag of clothes, and she did not remember what the name of the town she'd stopped in was. It did not matter very much as she had all of her money secreted in a hidden inner pocket of her coat.

As it happened though, exhausted, sore and ready for a large meal, Elizabeth stumbled back into the same market town, and purchased a large loaf of bread and some jerky from a bakery before going to the inn again for coffee and punch in the common room.

Somehow the world was a bit better.

Her mind returned to Darcy. Too many times.

Don't be a goose. This should not hurt. This should not hurt. This should not hurt.

Darcy's voice echoed in her mind, again and again: *You cannot expect me to choose against my judgement, my name, my very character.*

The vice squeezed her heart. Her eyes watered, and she swallowed all of the hot fruity rum punch she'd bought in a single gulp. Sadly Elizabeth could not drink herself into an oblivion alone here, without any friends for fifty miles, as far as she knew.

Despite her long walk, filled with signs to many streets, and a turnpike toll booth, whose signage *did* proclaim which direction was the way to London and that it was a little more than ninety-seven miles to the city, she only had a vague idea of exactly where she was and she did not want to ask.

It would be embarrassing, and she did not want to know.

Northern Northamptonshire or southern Leicestershire. That was her best guess. There were hundreds of towns this size in England, and even if she had travelled extensively, she would not know them all.

The next day Elizabeth's feet and legs hurt too much for her to walk again, and the day was grey and constantly rainy. She bought cheap off a traveller a novel he had finished reading and sat in the corner of the common room the entire day, looking out the window at sleeting rain, and watching the hypnotic flickering flames in the big grate.

She read nothing but the first page of the book. But she read that first page twenty times.

The next day Elizabeth again walked out, ignoring the muddy conditions, and she vigorously circled the entire area twice around. As Elizabeth returned from her energetic walk a loud angry shout rang out, "Elizabeth Bennet!" from the yard where the horses were changed. In that instant she cursed herself for not hiding *somewhere* that wasn't a coaching inn.

She cringed and ducked, as if that would do any good, before forcing herself to stand up and look to see who had called out her name. It had been a female voice. She simply hadn't expected to be hunted down seriously by anyone. Mr. Bennet would go to London for a week and then return home to his bookroom to sulk, while Mr. Darcy would be happy for the escape once he read her letter.

Georgiana Darcy had hitched up her skirts halfway to her knees and ran towards her with a fierce expression that made her look terrifyingly like her cousin Colonel Fitzwilliam.

"How dare you!" she shouted the instant she reached Elizabeth, waving her finger in Elizabeth's face. "How dare you break my brother's heart! How dare you leave him like that! How could you be so *wrong* to him! I thought you loved him! I thought you would be my friend! I thought you were worthy of my consideration. And then you ran away from... from *my brother*. I... I thought—" And suddenly the lioness was gone, and replaced by the doe once more. "Is it because of me? But I thought you loved Fitzwilliam. If you loved him, you wouldn't have ever left him. No matter what."

Her accusing eyes struck Elizabeth's heart. Suddenly all of the pain she'd suppressed, all of the sense of longing burst forward. Her eyes started leaking, and she asked desperately, "How is he? He cannot be too unhappy. Tell me, I must know how he does."

"No! No! No! You do not deserve to know. You left him. You don't love him. You hurt him. You left him heart broken—"

"Surely not, surely he isn't so very hurt. Tell me, Georgie, tell me how has he behaved."

"Mr. Darcy," Mrs. Annesley, who had caught up behind Georgiana at a sedate pace, "has been entirely committed to the search for you for the past days. He has been most taciturn about matters, and only said to us that he does not blame you, for—"

"She is the enemy!" Georgiana cried out, with a raging face again. "You do not share intelligence with the enemy! Cousin Richard taught me that! She left Fitzwilliam! She has no heart. She should — Lizzy why are you crying so much?"

"I do love him. I desperately love him. I had to leave him. Not for my own sake, but for his. I couldn't marry him, not with how I love him. But tell him that he need not worry for me. I thought he would not search for me. I explained everything in the letter. In the letter. But he is filled with honor, so he must think he has a duty to not simply let me run away — oh this is so terrible. He'll give up looking eventually."

"Lizzy, tell me, tell me why? Why would you ever leave Fitzwilliam if you love him?"

"Because he does not want to marry me, but he thinks he must."

"No! He loves you — what could ever make you think that?"

"Miss Bennet, I suspect matters are not so irretrievable as you and Miss Darcy seem to worry," Mrs. Annesley said, looking around at the crowd of people who were observing the two weeping women with interest.

Georgiana was now crying while she embraced the sobbing Elizabeth. "Perhaps we might continue in a private room. Have you been at that inn?" She pointed to the one where Elizabeth now saw one of Darcy's carriages having new horses hitched to it.

"He isn't here! Please tell me he is not. I cannot face him of a sudden."

"No dear, he isn't. He is questing after his lost maiden in London."

There was something comforting about the voice of the older woman, as though she had seen everything life might offer, or at least much of it, and she could manage any situation.

Elizabeth sniffingly nodded.

"You *shall* tell me the entire story. You need good advice. And tell Miss Darcy as well, what parts are appropriate for her — unless it is a matter you particularly think Mr. Darcy would wish to have hidden from his sister."

"What!" Georgiana looked dartingly between the other two women, curiosity overcoming her tears.

Her face flaming red, Elizabeth stutteringly replied as they walked towards the inn, "There is nothing *I* would blush to an excess to confess to *my* sisters. As for what Darcy wishes known... I cannot be certain."

"In that case you ought to tell her the entire story."

"What are you two talking about?"

They entered the main room of the inn. The innkeep looked with concern at Elizabeth at seeing her salty tear lined face, and with some interest at seeing her in the company of a young girl wearing a fine blue silk dress, fringed with expertly tatted lace, and with a large gold chain hanging from a pocket watch, and a jade hair pin encrusted with diamond.

Elizabeth had presented herself as genteel enough to the staff of the inn, but Georgiana was at a glance of a much higher sort of quality than her.

"Mr. Rockwell, might we have a private room to speak. My friends have just informed me of some news which... which..."

"Of course, Miss Hayes."

As the waiter led them to the upstairs room, Georgiana approvingly said, "Good tactics. Fitzwilliam has been asking around for Miss Smiths. But Cousin Richard said it was a waste of time, as you were too clever for that. Hayes is a *truly* unmemorable name."

"I hope no one of the name Hayes hears you saying that."

"You sound just like Fitzwilliam when you use that dry tone! Please tell me there is some hope still," Georgiana exclaimed.

"Do I?"

They were seated, tea was ordered, along with cold cuts, bread and several boiled eggs.

It was time to start speaking. To explain everything.

"Georgiana, it is not a waste of time for Mr. Darcy ask after Smith, since I could have decided that your brother would assume I am too clever to use the name, and then use it anyways."

"Miss Elizabeth," Mrs. Annesley said firmly. "Your story — might I assume there was some irregularity in the manner upon which your engagement was established? Not being a member of the family, I have heard some rumors from the servants..."

"Well, we... it was the rug's fault!"

"The rug's fault?"

"That bear rug. In the library. *You've* seen it. I tripped over it. That is how this all started."

"Ah!" There was a twinkle in Mrs. Annesley's eyes. "I think I conceive how matters must have gone. I stumbled over one of its claws, myself. Should be moved to a different room."

"Yes!"

Georgiana looked between the two women. "How does tripping over a rug lead to an engagement?"

Now Elizabeth's face turned red. "Ahem. Well."

"You ought to just say it. It does no good for the girl to think her brother *never* gets carried away — or you either. How far *did* matters go?"

"Just, well..." Elizabeth blushed. "Georgie, I must confess, remember when you said that Fitzwilliam was so disciplined that he could never be carried away by an improper passion, and I made a pretence of agreeing with you?"

The girl's eyes were wide, and her expression was one of the most intense fascination and curiosity.

"We were arguing, in the library at Netherfield — about Mr. Wickham, in fact, for I had not the wit to know at once that he was a worthless man. This was during a ball. And well, your brother is... he is in fact a passionate man, in which wells of feeling run deep, and I am as well."

"You kissed!" Georgiana delightedly grinned. "While arguing! It is so romantic."

"I am not sure," Mrs. Annesley said, "that I approve of such forms of romance as require conflict and argument, and such fires which couples claim to want. Mr. Annesley and I were the dearest of friends, and we rarely argued and never raised our voices to each other more than once or twice in the whole course of a year."

Georgiana rolled her eyes at her companion's worn wisdom. "Yes, yes. But not everyone is the same — what happened then! After you kissed, Lizzy."

"Well you must understand, I had no intention to kiss him. I think I already was in the path to loving your brother, but I believed, because he had — and here I must strike another blow against your belief in his perfection. May I?"

"Oh yes," Georgiana breathed out eagerly.

"He can be quite curmudgeonly and irritable at parties and balls."

"I knew *that* already."

"So the first words I ever heard from his mouth were when he and Bingley stood quite close to me at a ball. Bingley said, 'Darcy, good fellow, go dance with that dashedly pretty girl there.' And Mr. Darcy looked upon me, caught my eye, and then he turned coldly away, and said in a carrying voice, 'She is tolerable enough, but not handsome enough to tempt *me*.'"

"He didn't!"

"He did."

"Oh!" Georgiana clasped her hand over her mouth with horrified eyes. Then she giggled helplessly.

Elizabeth and Mrs. Annesley laughed along, and Elizabeth added, "So I naturally and immediately determined that I hated him forever."

"Yes!" Georgiana replied enthusiastically. "You tell the best stories about my brother! That is why you must marry him, so that you can tell me more!"

"Georgie—"

"I am sure that whatever the matter is that you are going to describe, is just a misunderstanding, or something easy to mend, and you two will be very happy together, and we'll all live at Pemberley until years and years from now, when I am at least almost as old as you, I get married. And then we'll visit each other."

Elizabeth was struck hard by this vision. And somehow... somehow she felt it might be true.

"So you were seen kissing?" Mrs. Annesley asked, returning them to the thread of the story. "Perhaps after you tripped over the bear rug?"

Elizabeth smiled, and somehow the pain of his rejection was lessened by knowing he'd spent the last days desperately hunting for her. He had said he loved her, even if he did not choose her. She became starry eyed as she remembered that moment, the whoop in her stomach as she flailed her arms forward, and then the feel of his hands around her waist, pulling her up. "He caught me, in his arms as I fell. And... we looked into each other's eyes, in the flickering candlelight."

Georgiana swooningly sighed.

"He held me there, tightly and strong, and he'd just rescued me from falling flat on my face, and—" Elizabeth sighed too. Even Mrs. Annesley sighed.

All three women stared ahead starry eyed.

"It was very romantic," Elizabeth concluded. "But then my mother burst into the library for some reason, with Mr. Bingley and Sir William behind her, and after we were seen kissing by three such people, and Mama started shouting that we were engaged... well we couldn't gracefully do anything but agree that we were to marry."

"But... after kissing like that," Georgiana asked. "Didn't you both want to marry?"

"At first? I was conflicted. I hated that I never had any choice. If I was to lose my independence... I wanted a choice." Elizabeth growled. "He never even *asked* me."

"What!" Georgiana was clearly horrified by this information, while Mrs. Annesley nodded in understanding and took a bite from the biscuits the inn had provided while sipping her tea.

"You *shouldn't* marry him, not until he properly asks you! I am shocked. I thought Fitzwilliam would do better than that to a woman he loves as much as you. But that was no reason to just run away without telling him you needed him to ask you first. He would have."

And then the vice was clamped around her chest again. *My character. My judgement. My very nature. I don't choose you.* "I did! The night before the wedding. When your uncle was at the dinner, and Colonel Fitzwilliam entertained us all, and there was all the dancing, and then — we hid in the library to talk, and to remember how we had become engaged. It is impossible to not love your brother desperately. So I told him. I told him I loved him, and I asked him if he would... would..."

"Poor dear." Mrs. Annesley put her hand on Elizabeth's arm comfortingly.

"I asked if he would choose to marry me if we were both free. And he said that even though he loved me, my connections were too low, and his judgement would rebel against it, and he would not have made an offer for me if we were free. So that was *his* choice. What he said."

Georgiana clenched her fists together. "That bastard. He *does* deserve to suffer like Richard said he does."

"So you see why I couldn't marry him."

All three women sadly stared at the teapot and their tea cups.

Mrs. Annesley poured Elizabeth a new cup, filling hers to the brim. "Drink up, dear. You've had a hard time of it. But this is... not quite a misunderstanding. But something similar. I think Mr. Darcy only needs a little time to miss you and realize that he has been quite an idiot. Men can be slow to think and truly understand themselves. I will be quite surprised if in the end you and he do not make a match of it, though."

"Really?" Elizabeth hopefully gazed into the older woman's eyes. "Truly, you think that — oh, but I fear to hope."

"I am certain. But you can't meet Mr. Darcy again *yet*. He needs more time to think and realize how much he loves you first. Best you come with us, so we can keep you safe until the time comes. We'll show you Pemberley — Georgie will like that very much, for her to be the one to take you round the walks — and we'll tell everyone that you are my niece who is visiting with me after your father died — except Mr. Tom our coachman, and Mrs. Reynolds the housekeeper will need to hear the truth. I don't doubt that Mr. Darcy gave orders to watch the watcher after what Mrs. Younge did."

Chapter Fourteen

"You are Miss Bennet?" Mrs. Reynold's wrinkled face was tight and stiff with anger. "The girl who jilted our Mr. Darcy. I do not think we want someone like you here. No matter what you've convinced Miss Darcy of. But I will send him a letter—"

"He deserved it!" Georgiana pounded her fist against her hand. "I never would have *believed* it of Fitzwilliam."

"The master?" Mrs. Reynold's looked at Georgiana. "I very much doubt that."

"He did! He told her that he didn't want to marry her. That's why Lizzy left. Just because she wasn't rich, like we are."

Mrs. Reynolds touched the back of her neck, right below the bun of grey hair. She wrinkled her eyebrows together. "What occurred? That does not sound like something that Mr. Darcy would say."

"I know! It was terrible. And he *does* want to marry her. And he admires Elizabeth so much. I even saw them kiss, and—"

"What!" Elizabeth screeched. "When?"

Georgiana blushed and waved her hand side to side. "Richard told me where to watch, and—"

"*Richard* watched us kiss!" Elizabeth's voice was now quite high pitched.

"That is not the point. And after I saw them kiss, in a way that clearly showed true love and—"

"What were we doing?" Elizabeth squeaked or squealed.

"And he loves her so much, I cannot *believe* Fitzwilliam would keep me from having Lizzy as a sister!"

Mrs. Reynolds now was openly smiling at the younger girl. "I doubt very much *that* was the purpose to which he intended his behavior."

"Of course *not*. Because Fitzwilliam wasn't thinking. He can be as much a fool as me. I rather like knowing that."

Mrs. Annesley said, "That does not mean you should not listen to him, or to others around you."

Georgiana rolled her eyes. "Of course not! It proves everyone needs to listen to other people, because even very clever and kind older brothers can be complete fools when they are in love."

"He really was not so bad as you makes him sound..." Elizabeth cautiously said.

"So, young lady." Mrs. Reynolds looked her over determinedly. "I expect you to tell me the story."

"Uh..." The older woman's gaze could be quite intimidating. Elizabeth wondered if she had learned it from Mr. Darcy, or, if, more likely, Mr. Darcy had learned it from her. "We had not intended to become engaged. I..." Elizabeth really could not tell the story to the clear blue eyes and solid distinguished face of the reliable old servant.

"She tripped and fell into his arms!" Georgiana chimed up enthusiastically. "And then they looked into each other's eyes and kissed. Isn't the story excessively romantic? It makes me gush just to hear Lizzy tell it!"

"Ah." Mrs. Reynolds smiled, looking at Elizabeth with something more like friendliness. "And you were not trying to entrap the master in any way."

"Of course she wasn't!"

"Georgie." The mildly reproving voice let her quiet. "It is Miss Bennet's place to defend herself, not yours."

"I did not." There was a pause. "That we are not married is ample proof, I think, of that."

"Why did you not marry him?"

"I asked, the night before we were to marry if he would choose to marry me if we were free. He said he would not. And I..." Elizabeth took a shallow pained breath. She still could not say it calmly. "So I then..."

"See! Lizzy is crying again." Georgiana stood with her hands on her hips. "And she is going to stay here with me, as my dear and *particular* friend, until Fitzwilliam has suffered long enough to make up for what he said to her, and then we'll tell him, and he'll come back, and they will marry, and everyone will live happily forever!" She stamped her foot and pointed her finger in Mrs. Reynold's eye. "I won't let you stop me."

"Of course not, Georgie. I shall have a room prepared for..."

"Miss Hayes," Mrs. Annesley replied. "My niece."

"Miss Hayes. A solid unremarkable name — but not forever. I will tell the master eventually."

"No! I don't want to make him marry me."

"Miss Bennet, no one has ever, not even his father, been able to make Mr. Darcy do anything he particularly did not want to do. It was a good thing he was the sweetest and most even tempered and well-behaved boy as a child. Because with his stubbornness, he would have been a terror if he were prone to misbehavior."

And like that "Miss Hayes" gained a place at Pemberley. And she loved it.

To think she *might* be the mistress of this estate one day.

Georgiana's unfailing optimism began to eat into her. Darcy's face, his kisses. What he had said, when he said he ardently admired her. Surely,

surely... surely he would realize he loved her more than those other considerations after enough time had passed that she could reveal herself to him once more without binding him in any way.

Elizabeth heard many stories of Mr. Darcy and his childhood from Mrs. Reynolds. Dear stories about a boy who adored his mother, who was the finest lady to ever live in these parts. Stories about Darcy making a mess of his clothes while playing around in the lakes and streams with Richard and Wickham and other friends. Stories about how much he loved his father.

And there were stories about how he rode over all of Pemberley's lands as a young lad, seeking to know all the people and all the fields and hedges that would be his. She heard stories about Mr. Darcy as a master, showing kindness to those who fell behind on their rents due to illness or disability, while firmly and evenly dealing with those who tried to cheat him or others.

Fitzwilliam Darcy was the best man, the best master, the best landlord anyone could imagine.

Though, stubborn.

Everyone agreed he was stubborn when he set his mind to it.

On one of her walks Elizabeth met one of the gardeners, an old white-haired man with half fingered gloves doing some outdoors work on the unseasonably warm day. Elizabeth asked him about his work, and then, as had become her habit, she asked him about how Mr. Darcy was thought of.

She liked to hear people say nice things about Mr. Darcy, and everyone did when she asked.

"Best master in all of Derbyshire. Everyone knows it. I have the jealousy of everyone in the public house when they know where I have a position. I've been settled here quite long. Know the plants inside and out. Have a cottage here, warm, spacious, and he never cheats us on the rent. I always have ample for both the necessities and all the little luxuries that a workman can want — I can't understand it."

"What?"

"Wait..." He eyed Elizabeth skeptically. "Didn't they say you from Hertfordshire?"

"I cannot honestly disclaim the connection. That is where I was born and bred."

"Huh." He now peered at her with a great deal of suspicion. "Like *that* woman. The one who went and broke the master's heart. They say, those of us who've seen him in London, that he has ridden back and forth everywhere looking for her. And after she *jilted* him. Just goes to show what sort of man he is."

"It does," Elizabeth replied, choked with some emotion. "But surely—"

"There you go. Defending her, just because you are from the same county. But Mr. Darcy should have known better than to court a southerner — just goes to show what happens when you have truck with folk near London. They aren't any good, never, never, never."

He then glared at Elizabeth daring her to contradict him.

She had time to recollect her emotions, and when she replied she said, "I have never had a truer description of my home county's deficiencies. This is in fact why I left and I hope to settle in a more sensible location. In these parts in fact."

"You do?" The old gardener gave her a skeptical look. "Well, you'll be a credit to us if you do. But sure you don't want to stay near London? Everyone always goes to as 'prentices, or to see the world, or quality like yourself for the season. I won't. Never been further off than that tall hill a mile past Lambton in my life, and don't plan to go even that far again."

"A constrained life. You do not want for more?"

"I don't think I do. Kind of you to ask. There was a different lady. Visited here twice. She was convinced I had no idea about anything. So I just sort of played along. Sister of that happy fellow — some men said she was angling for the master. He was too clever for her though. Just goes to show that even if a family is from the north, they can be rotten. We should mostly only deal with good Derby stock. This girl did spend a great deal of time at *school* in London. Must be where—"

"Is this Miss Bingley we are speaking of?"

"You know her, Ma'am! Apologies. Apologies. I ought not go on about my betters like this. Ought not. But at my age, the master'll never dismiss me. He is too kind. But apologies." He pulled his white forelock.

Elizabeth laughed. "I dislike her at least as much as you do. At least as much."

"Heh. Did you know that Miss Bennet, the one who broke the master's heart? I'd like to give *her* a talking to."

"I would too," Elizabeth said seriously. "I will confess, we were on terms of some intimacy, and it was *her* behavior which principally convinced me I should depart from Hertfordshire. I could never understand a woman who does not admire a man such as Mr. Darcy. He is the finest gentleman I have ever met."

"That's a proper attitude." The gardener worked his hoe with several more whacks at the cold ground. "It's a shame this Miss Bennet did not think more like you, Ma'am. A roaring shame."

"One should not judge too deeply into the hearts of others, without knowing the particulars, but I dare to say you are right."

"Glad the little miss has you for a friend, Ma'am. She gets lonely she does."

And with that the gardener finished his work, tugged his cap downward in respect once more, and the two separated.

Georgiana was delightful, and Elizabeth had already decided that she treasured her — whether they would ever be sisters or not — more than Lydia at least.

One day while they sat in the drawing room, after Georgiana's hours of daily practice upon the piano, Georgiana asked Elizabeth, as she sat on the sofa reading a stiff backed book she had collected from the two-storied beautiful library, "I have been wondering. And you know so much..."

"Yes, Georgie?"

"When someone elopes, why do they call it marrying over the anvil?"

"That is a strange question. Neither of us are the eloping sort."

Georgiana grinned at her. "Not any more. It was something Wickham said to me — when I was younger and still the eloping sort."

Elizabeth laughed. "You still are younger."

Georgiana laughed. "Wickham talked about us going to marry over the anvil, and I asked what that meant. He laughed and didn't say, and I felt too embarrassed to ask further. But it has confused me ever since, and I've never had the bravery to query. I know they are poorer in Scotland. Do blacksmiths work in Scottish churches because the churches need to rent out space to survive?"

Elizabeth laughed kindly. "No. Not at all. Or at least not that I know. *I* have never been to Scotland either, you understand. And they are Presbyterians, with no bishops and a great few other differences. But I doubt they have blacksmiths operating from very many churches."

Georgiana scooted forward on the window seat, closer to Elizabeth. "So why? It sounded very bizarre to *me* as well."

"You see, this goes back to the whole reason you could marry in Scotland. Their church has different rules about the enactment of marriages. And one of their rules is that if two witnesses observe a marriage, it is valid. So suppose you are a couple who has travelled all of the way to Scotland, and your angry father—"

"Or well-intentioned and wonderful brother who wishes to stop you from making a terrible mistake because he adores you and cares deeply for your wellbeing and would make an excellent husband for *any* woman who is clever and who I like." Georgiana interrupted with her eyes bright. "Even if he is sometimes very foolish."

"Or your... ah." Elizabeth tilted her head as she puzzled out Georgiana's sentence. "Or your brother, is right behind you — to prevent you from making a terrible mistake. I think we can both agree that eloping, as a general rule, is a bad choice."

Georgiana nodded. "It always was in my head that it was wrong."

"Because you *are* a clever young lady."

Georgina smiled and waved her hand dismissively. "Back to the marriage over the anvil. What does Presbyterianism have to do with *that*?"

"Anyone can witness the marriage, and it makes it official if there are two such witnesses. I don't know why. It doesn't make any sense to me why the 'Kirk' thinks that anyone should be allowed to establish a marriage. You need a member of the clergy in *ordinary* countries. But they are nearly barbarians in Scotland, wearing kilts and speaking that strange not quite English language of theirs. It makes sense to me that the parties themselves, rather than their parents or their friends and other relatives should decide whether they may marry. So odd and unseemly habits, or not, in the end, *I* approve of Scotland."

"But what does that have to do with blacksmiths?"

"You arrive over the border and who is the first person who you know you will be able to find?"

"The innkeeper?"

Elizabeth threw up her hands. "What if there is no inn? Except I am sure there is an inn at Gretna Green since so many silly young couples go through there. So I do not know why it is 'marry over the anvil' rather than 'Marry over the beer tap'."

"It does sound," Georgiana said reflectively, with twinkling eyes, "more romantic to marry over an anvil than over a beer tap."

"That depends on how much affection you hold for beer."

Georgiana laughed. "Well I shall marry in a church. Or in the drawing room here at Pemberley if we get a special license."

"And I shall not marry at all, having come so close to the parson's mousetrap — I mean the blacksmith's beartrap — I shall assiduously avoid all interactions with men for the remainder of my life."

Georgiana stuck her tongue out.

"Fine, only until I am such a spinster old maid that *men* assiduously avoid interactions with me."

Chapter Fifteen

Despite Colonel Fitzwilliam's effort to convince him it was pointless, Darcy spent three weeks first hunting through respectable, but cheap London boarding houses, and then up and down the roads round about the countryside, hunting for any sign of where Elizabeth had gone.

He wanted to see her.

He dreamed of her each night. And he *was* worried.

But there was no sign or hint of her. The closest he came was in the town of Shoby where a girl had stayed there for three days under the name of Miss Hayes.

She matched Elizabeth's description and tendency to read and walk great distances, but she had left in a fine carriage, and she had been remembered after two weeks by many of the local regulars at the inn because they had guessed she was running from, or maybe towards, some gentleman. Darcy had been hopeful until he learned that Miss Hayes had left the town with some rich young lady, whose name nobody could remember, in a giant four horse carriage. No one knew where they went, and anyways, Elizabeth would have stayed in place, or taken the stage coach.

Darcy called on the townhouse of the Matlocks early in the morning before Richard rode out to his duty with the regiment. "Please. Cousin. I have failed on my own. I beg you to help me search for Elizabeth."

Colonel Fitzwilliam tilted his head. "Getting bit thin. You haven't cared for yourself very well."

"I at least haven't been thrown from my horse onto my head, like you predicted I would."

"Said it worried me, not that you would. Fine rider. I know you are."

Colonel Fitzwilliam picked up his newspaper again and shook it out. "Fine news coming from Russia these days. The little ogre has frozen half his army to death. Deuced fine news."

"Hang Napoleon!"

"Yes, I hope they do. And I hope I am there when it happens. We are to be sent back to Spain soon. Need to finish them off."

"Oh, I thought Uncle had convinced them that real soldiers were needed for the London regiments."

"Eh, and I convinced them I was needed in Spain again. Going to get a general's hat with the next list."

"Congratulations." Darcy grinned. "You deserve it."

"Will be less fun commanding a division than a regiment. But I do what the kingdom demands."

"Elizabeth. Before you go back to Spain, you must help me find her."

"Now I have told you... seven times now. Yes seven. She will appear when she is ready."

"She *hasn't*!"

Colonel Fitzwilliam shrugged. "Ah, men in love. Impatient. But one must not charge before the moment is present for victory to be achieved. Not even though the canons are raking through your waiting soldiers. You must wait till that key time on which all depends and—""

"Dash it! I wonder why I ask you for help."

"Because I am the most capable man you know, including yourself. Which is high praise."

"I haven't been capable of finding Elizabeth."

"Because she has not been where you looked."

Darcy sat down stiffly, and grabbed a fork and savagely stabbed a piece of sausage from the platter in the center of the table. "I hate this. I hate it. I never knew myself till I knew Elizabeth. I hate this waiting."

Colonel Fitzwilliam snorted, but made no further reply as he turned himself back to his breakfast.

"You do not understand. You have never been in love. You have never made such a mistake that it tortures your soul and that you feel the pain every day of knowing the mistake, and knowing that you have hurt another, and just desperately hoping, hoping to make it better by being able to speak to her once. You cannot understand."

"I understand in part," Colonel Fitzwilliam replied with distant eyes. "I too have hurt others. I have made mistakes, and — I do not know what it is to be in love. But I have made mistakes of greater moment than *that* upon that field of battle. Those mistakes which made men — men who I knew — to die unnecessarily. And I have had to grieve them, and live with the ghosts taking irregular occasions to return haunting me to ensure that I still remember that this man is dead, and that this man's dying breath had been my fault."

Darcy had nothing to say to that. It... gave him some perspective. He let out a long breath and stared at the decorative pattern on the breakfast table.

"Pemberley," Colonel Fitzwilliam unexpectedly added, after a period of silence.

"What?"

"Go home. To Pemberley. See Georgiana. See your house. You came for my help, and that is my advice. Go home to Pemberley."

"I can't. Not while Elizabeth is still missing, and..."

"Your hunting randomly will not find her. But... I think an answer you seek. You will find an answer at Pemberley."

Colonel Fitzwilliam stood up and wiped a last bit of the breakfast butter from the edge of his lips. "You will no doubt ignore this advice. You are generally set in your own stratagems and plans. But go to Pemberley. All I am willing to say. I recommend Pemberley as strongly as I can. And now I am off to my own duties."

Darcy returned to his townhouse in London. He felt like crying.

Every day he remembered Elizabeth trembling, and every day he cursed himself as an idiot, for not yet seeing that day that he would do anything, *anything* to marry her.

Darcy sat in his study. It snowed outside, the soft white floating lovely, like wheat being slowly sifted, to the ground. He usually loved to watch the snow from his window. He was warm and well fed, with tea and coffee, and chocolates and alcohol and every substance of pleasure a man could order at his fingertips.

He just wanted to share it with Elizabeth.

Good Elizabeth, sweet Elizabeth, lovely and kind Elizabeth. And she had destroyed her position in the community, and with her father, and, she believed, with him, all to save him from a marriage he claimed not to want. To protect his honor from needing to marry her.

She was the best of women.

Suddenly, without expecting it, Darcy found himself on his knees, praying.

Dear Jehovah above, he thought, *please protect her, and keep her happy and laughing wherever she is. And I beg you, give me a chance to see her once more.*

When Darcy rose stiffly back to his feet some time later, after his knees had ached with a pain that he welcomed as a form of penance, he had decided: he would return to Pemberley, like Colonel Fitzwilliam had suggested.

Chapter Sixteen

"You have a very great lot of dresses."

There were more silks and sashes and muslins and Cashmirs and petticoats, and every form of clothing in the giant closet than Elizabeth had ever seen in one place in her life, including in a dressmaker's shop.

"I know! Yet I never have anything to wear! It is absurd."

Elizabeth laughed. "What do you want to appear as?"

"I do not know — some of these may fit you, Lizzy. I have not thrown them out as I kept getting taller and taller. Quite not the fashion anymore. I hear that everywhere."

"You are very much a fashionable figure for *me*."

"Yes, but I'm too tall. And we aren't even certain yet that I have stopped growing."

Elizabeth grinned. "What you need is a few simple pieces you like very much — that is the key to how Jane and I always look so beautiful. We do not have more than a half dozen really good dresses, but the ones we do have complement us exceedingly well. Yours... well these are almost immodest—"

"The ones Mrs. Younge suggested," Georgiana agreed with a disgusted expression.

"If you never intend to touch them, you should offer them out as charity."

Georgiana hugged Elizabeth. "I can do that? I felt as if... it would be somehow wasteful to simply get rid of dresses."

"Yes, many people like to have a chance to touch and use finer silks."

"Then I will do that!"

"And these," Elizabeth pointed to the other section of the closet, the one with the dresses she had seen Georgiana wear several times. "They are..."

"Dowdy! *Too* modest. And no *je ne sais quoi*. Not like your clothes. You wear everything so *perfect*."

"Yes... hmmmm. They can be trimmed into something that I think will fit you very well."

"Trimmed... can the modiste in the town do this, or must we return to London, and—"

Elizabeth laughed. "Have you never modified your own dresses?"

"No! Oh this is so exciting."

"It can be a great deal of work — though if any of your maids are versed in fine needlework we can ask them to help and direct them."

Georgiana almost bounced quiveringly. "So exciting. So exciting. So exciting."

"Now which dress should we work on — there is always a chance we make a mistake and ruin the dress so I think this one." Elizabeth pulled a little forward a finely cut woolen dress which she had never seen Georgiana wear, and that showed every sign of having been chosen for the girl by a clergyman's widow: Specifically Mrs. Annesley. Georgiana's companion was a woman for whose character Elizabeth had the highest respect, but she was not a master of fashion.

"You can fix it so it is not ugly!"

"*We* can fix it!"

"Lizzy! You are the best friend I have ever had!"

Such a statement required that Elizabeth hug her dear friend tightly. "You are a very dear, dear friend — I refuse to insult other dear friends by claiming them less than you. But you are as dear to me as anyone else I have ever known."

"Really?" Georgiana glowed.

"I would be very happy to switch you with Lydia."

Georgiana laughed. "That isn't a very surprising choice. I am *much* sweeter than Lydia."

They smiled at each other.

Such happiness and intensity of friendship required a moment of panic to follow.

There were sharp knocks on the door, and a strained voice very familiar to both of them came through the wood. "Georgie, Georgie," Mr. Darcy said, "I have just arrived back from searching for Elizabeth. Might I enter?"

Elizabeth's eyes widened. She frantically shook her head as Georgiana opened her mouth. "Don't tell him," she said in a rushed whisper.

"But—" Georgie said back as Elizabeth clasped her hand over Georgie's mouth.

Elizabeth looked frantically around.

Darcy knocked on the door again, "Georgie, I was told you were within?"

"I... I am fine. A moment, brother."

"Into the closet!" Georgiana whispered frantically.

Elizabeth opened the door and went to hide within, but drew back. She said very quietly shaking her head, "I'd wrinkle the dresses."

Georgiana tensely whispered back, "Don't be ridiculous."

Elizabeth dropped to the floor and then shimmied backwards under Georgiana's bed. The girl's eyes widened and then she grinned and with an expression of general mischief once Elizabeth had fully hidden under the bed. She opened the door to her brother.

Fitzwilliam Darcy's legs walked into the room. That was all Elizabeth could see of him as he paced restlessly.

Georgiana queried with a smile in her voice, "I am glad to see you so *sudden* — we got no note that you would return. Unexpected."

Darcy continued to pace, giving Elizabeth an excellent view of his tall riding boots, and sometimes, when he stepped close to the window on the opposite side of the room from the bed, she could also see his tan riding breeches wrapped around his finely shaped calves. The area under the bed was not in fact dusty, there were no spider webs, and everything seemed entirely clean.

When she escaped her present predicament, Elizabeth needed to deliver her compliments to the maid who cleaned Georgiana's room, and to Mrs. Reynolds for her fine instruction and management of the staff. In her childhood visits to beneath beds in Longbourn during games of sardines, she had discovered that *their* beds did certainly have dust and spider webs, and similar matters that a girl of eight, or at least Elizabeth at the age of eight, delighted in.

"I was advised," Darcy said at last, "to return to Pemberley by Richard. I cannot find her. She has disappeared entirely. And until she chooses to be found, I cannot find her."

"Richard?" Georgiana had a sly tone to her voice, and Elizabeth suspected that Georgiana had sent her favorite cousin the knowledge of Elizabeth's presence at Pemberley.

"The man absolutely refused to help me look for Elizabeth in any practical way." Darcy paced back to the bed and sat on it, his weight making the mattress to press Elizabeth uncomfortably into the ground so that she could barely breathe. In compensation she was able to look at the back of his ankles from five inches distance. Elizabeth rather liked the trade.

From how Darcy settled himself, Elizabeth thought he was putting his face in his hands.

"Fitzwilliam," Georgiana said with what Elizabeth recognized as a *faux* angry tone, "I cannot understand why you are so committed to finding Lizzy — I mean Miss Bennet. Miss Bennet. She left you! With no provocation, no... reason to leave you, when you desperately *wanted* to marry her, and kept telling her how much you wanted to marry. And then she left you because..."

"Oh Georgiana! I wronged Elizabeth. You shall never believe, seeing me as you do, how I failed the woman who I love most."

"Fitzwilliam, what did you do! There is nothing you could say which would justify a girl *choosing* to not marry you, after she accepted your *offer*."

The girl was laying it on a bit thick. Elizabeth would need to coach her a bit more upon subtlety.

Darcy caught no sense that Georgiana was making fun of him as he groaned and stood up. "Georgie, I... I told her I did not want to marry her." Darcy walked to the window and stared out. Or at least Elizabeth thought he did, as after all she could barely see the tops of his knees.

He sighed.

Elizabeth's heart seized. What would he say next?

"But you do?" Georgiana's almost worried voice caught Elizabeth's feel of anxiety as well.

"Desperately," Darcy replied with a sigh. "I want to marry her more desperately than anything I have ever wanted. More than... Jove, I have been a fool. Such a fool. From the very first a fool. I cannot tell you the particulars, but... from the very first I pretended to myself I did not wish to marry Elizabeth, when she is the most beautiful, the most perfect, the sweetest, the kindest, the most honorable, the most clever, the most — I love her. If I can only find her, and tell her."

Elizabeth's heart pattered quickly. Did Darcy truly think this of her?

Georgiana cheerily asked, "Imagine Elizabeth is here, right now in this room, what would you say to her?"

"I would say to her that I ardently admire and love her — No, I already said that once to her and then I broke her heart — the kindest, sweetest, most tender heart in the world."

Darcy sat on the bed again. For a long time. Five or six strained breaths. Elizabeth really would have preferred it if he planned out sweet things to say while *not* sitting on top of her.

He stood up again. "She is my choice. Always my choice. My one true choice. I would tell her that I was wrong. My judgement before was ill judged, every word I spoke against her family, her position, and about the importance of seeking wealth and connections. It made me no better than a Candlebacon, I mean a Wickham. I would tell her that I know better now, and that if she would only let me, I would spend my entire life proving to her that I choose her."

"Awwww." Georgiana's voice swooned. "That was beautifully said."

And then Elizabeth sneezed.

"Achoo! Achoo! Achoo!"

Whatever got into her nose took three powerful, and slightly painful, trapped in tight conditions under the bed, sneezes to clear.

When she stopped sneezing, she found herself staring from inches away into Mr. Darcy's clear beautiful eyes as he'd knelt down to look under the bed.

*****

Darcy had imagined many times what it would be like when he at last met Elizabeth again. How she would look at him, what she would say, how he would convince her to marry him. The fantasy of finding Elizabeth had been one he'd contemplated many, many times.

On occasion this fantasy ended with both of them *sans vêtements*.

However, despite having imagined meeting Elizabeth at least a hundred times in the past month, he had *never*, not even once, contemplated the possibility that she would be hidden under his sister's bed.

The two rather awkwardly stared at each other. Some deeply ingrained instinct made him say, "Miss Bennet! How do you do?"

"More passion!" Georgiana exclaimed.

Elizabeth coughed again, and she tried to slither forward, and extended her hand out towards him. "I cannot get myself free of this bed."

"I told you to hide in the closet," Georgiana said, kneeling next to Darcy. "Who cares if the clothes get crumpled?"

Darcy took Elizabeth's arm with a firm grip upon her elbow and then he counted to three, and pulled her forward, till she was mostly out from under the bed.

Elizabeth lay gasping on the floor for a minute red faced as she pulled her legs — very pretty legs whose white stockings were on ample view — back under her.

"Last time I'll hide under a bed," she exclaimed sourly.

"It is easier playing hide-and-find as a child," Darcy agreed as he offered her a hand to help her stand.

And then they were standing there, once more inches from each other's faces. And they looked into each other's eyes. The desire was still there in Elizabeth's eyes. It was still there in his eyes.

And then, as they leaned forward to kiss, drawn by that passion neither of them could control, Darcy caught sight of Georgiana grinning in the corner of the room.

Georgiana was grinning too widely.

She'd known Elizabeth was there, and made him to say what he felt about her just so that Elizabeth could hear.

Georgiana had known.

This entire time while he'd been desperately searching for Elizabeth, Georgiana had known and kept her hidden from him here at Pemberley.

"How could you do this to me?"

Georgiana got that mulish face that reminded Mr. Darcy of Papa when he was determined to stand upon principles. "You made your *choice* clear to Lizzy. I wasn't going to interfere with what *you* wanted."

"You *knew* I was looking for her and—"

Elizabeth took his hand and squeezed it softly. "May I apologize for leaning upon your house's hospitality without properly asking permission? I did not want... I could not yet face you."

And once more, it was as though Georgiana was not present in the room.

"You heard me just now. Elizabeth, I have spoken what is in my heart, and in my soul, and I will repeat it once more, and again and again, until you understand, I choose you. Always, forever. In every way you. It is you, your beautiful soul, your sweet loving dedication to what is right, your way of laughing and seeing through me, the happiness I feel next to you. I choose you, every time."

"I heard you, but you hurt me. I... I have never felt so bad as I did that night."

"I know. I shall always live with that memory. Every day since the way you looked has tormented me. Even that night — I realized, somehow during my dreams, I knew I wanted to marry you, that night I chose it. I think even as you sneaked subtly from Longbourn, I knew that I would choose to marry you and—"

"Why couldn't you have known *then*! When I *asked* you. Why? Why? Why?"

"Oh, Lizzy. I..." He did not have anything to say which sounded sufficient as an excuse in his own ears. "I was a cursed fool."

She was still holding his hand.

Darcy pulled his Elizabeth to himself, holding her against his chest, with his arm around her. She sweetly breathed, a perfect weight in his arms.

Georgiana was still grinning at him. Like she had all along. Darcy gestured with his head for her to leave the room. She shook her head and mouthed, "Chaperone."

Darcy mouthed back, as Elizabeth still clung to him, crying, and while he brushed his hands along the smooth cotton back of her indoors dress, "I don't need a chaperone."

Georgiana shrugged and threw her hands in the air. She mouthed back, exaggerating the motion of her lips, "What?"

"I don't need a chaperone." This time Darcy spoke aloud.

Elizabeth wetly giggled and looked up at him. Her eyes sparkled with tears and glowed with love. "If there *ever* has been a couple who needed a chaperone, it was us."

He wanted to kiss her. By Jove even here, in his sister's bedroom, in front of his sister, he wanted to kiss her.

"You mean it?" Elizabeth asked. "Do you truly mean it?"

"Not one day, not one hour has passed since you parted from me when I did not think of you. My dreams have been filled with your kisses, my days have been filled with longing and worry — I have been so anxious for you. I was terrified, Bingley and Colonel Fitzwilliam insisted — *wait a minute*. Richard knew. He must have known. Him too?"

Darcy looked rather betrayed.

Elizabeth giggled, her wonderful happy sound. "I have been betrayed as well, since I thought my presence here was only to be known by Georgiana, Mrs. Annesley and Mrs. Reynolds, and I also surmised during the past half hour that *another* was informed."

"Well?"

"Aren't you both glad I told him?"

Darcy was.

At least if Elizabeth was.

He looked at her. Close in the eyes. "Are you happy?"

"You never even asked me to marry you! Do you remember, I was told we were to marry, but you never made a proposal." She sounded exasperated.

"Ah. I see that you acted most properly then," Darcy replied with a smile. "I would not marry a man who had not proposed to me either."

Elizabeth grinned back at him. "*You* would not marry a man at all."

"Elizabeth Bennet." Darcy knew what she was inviting him to do. At least he desperately hoped that she wanted him to do this. He kneeled on the rug in front of her, and took both her soft hands between his hands. He laced their fingers together, and his heart bumped as much at this intimacy as it would at a kiss.

"Dearest, sweetest, Elizabeth. My love, my life, my choice. I wish to spend my life with you, I wish you to be the companion of my days, and the mother of my children, and the one who I hold each night, and the woman who fills my life with brightness and joy from her laughter. You are my choice. The only choice I want to make. Every fragment of my being longs for you. And it is no hyperbole when I say that if you accept my hand, I shall be the happiest man in England."

Elizabeth said nothing for a moment. She shyly lowered her eyes, and then looked directly into his eyes again. "Yes. Fitzwilliam, yes. I... Yes!"

Darcy rose to his feet, and pulled Elizabeth into his arms and kissed her.

Their kiss was interrupted by Georgiana pumping her fist and shouting, "Yes!"

Chapter Seventeen

Elizabeth continued to live as "Miss Hayes" at Pemberley, but the illusion for the staff was now quite thin. An express was sent off immediately to Mr. Bennet, asking for his permission for them to marry, and Darcy acquired from the bishop in Derby a license to allow them to marry as soon as he received Mr. Bennet's permission, which was necessary as Elizabeth was still twenty.

The two of them *really* wanted to be married at this point.

It was impossible, entirely impossible, for an honorable gentleman, in his own home, to anticipate his wedding vows with a guest of his sister.

Elizabeth was not happy about that, but she agreed entirely that Georgiana did deserve a good example from them. And so they spent the entire following days while the waited for Mr. Bennet's reply looking longingly at each other while they read books in the library, went on long winter walks, worked on modifying Georgiana's dresses — well only Elizabeth did the last. Darcy sat in the room watching while pretending to write letters of business.

Georgiana was too eager to have the dress for Elizabeth to just stare longingly at Darcy, unfortunately.

They sat near enough to bump knees during every meal, and the house was decidedly off limits to visitors.

Those five days of waiting were as idyllic as any period of time that did not involve already actually being married and sharing a bed could be. Elizabeth even suspected that she would, in years to come, look back on this brief period of courtship with a great deal of nostalgia.

However at present her main emotion was a desire to explore those desires that Darcy's regular embraces and kisses woke and strengthened.

This delightful period was shattered when Mr. Bennet arrived at Pemberley five days after Darcy.

He'd taken the heavy Longbourn carriage, which looked far worse for the wear of being rushed up the roads to Derbyshire over just a few days. Papa's sideburns were ruffled, and it was clear from his appearance that he had not bathed or paused for three days.

When they went out to the front to meet him, he pointed his walking stick at Darcy. "You! Pretending to have no idea where Lizzy was!"

"Mr. Bennet, I am very glad to—"

"No! A thousand times no! Both of you. No. I'll never give my permission again to you to take my Lizzy. Elizabeth, you are coming home with me. Now!"

"Papa, I love Mr. Darcy, and—"

"Nonsense! This is just a mad passion like what I felt for your mother. Infatuation makes you stupid over his fine appearance, and tall form, like I swooned over your mother's... No! You'll not marry him. No. A thousand times. No. No *ten* thousand times, no!"

"I want to marry him. And—"

"You are yet my daughter. And you will remain my daughter. I don't think I will *ever* give you permission to marry anyone. You don't have the spirit for it."

Mr. Bennet's ranting voice echoed across the wide dale that Pemberley was set in. Darcy hurried up next to Mr. Bennet, keeping himself between Elizabeth and her father. "Please, sir. I have made many mistakes and—"

"You disgraceful man. Hiding my daughter on your estate! All the while pretending to search London for her and—"

"I had no notion she was here."

Georgiana hurried up, and anxiously said, "Mr. Bennet, please, I brought Lizzy here. And aren't you glad she was safe? But she and Fitzwilliam need to marry. Can't you see that they need to? They love each other. I saw him propose, this time, and it was so romantic, and—"

"Dash it, girl." Mr. Bennet growled. "You are no more sensible than my Lydia. No more."

Georgiana drew back with a decidedly offended expression on her face. "I am too."

"Not a whit. All girls are silly things that need to be protected from men, and never given a chance to run their way into trouble. Less sensible, the female sex. And, Lizzy, you are coming home *now*."

So saying, Mr. Bennet grabbed Elizabeth by the arm, who pulled her elbow away from her father.

Mr. Darcy harshly said, "I would ask you to not handle my wife in such a way."

"Your wife? No, she is not. This is England, and you cannot marry a girl of her age without her father's support. Will you come with me, Lizzy, or must I bring a magistrate to demand you from your kidnapper?"

Elizabeth looked between Papa and Darcy. "You'll wait for me? It is only another six months till I am of age."

"Ha, you plan to marry without my permission then?"

"Papa. I plan to live my entire life with Mr. Darcy."

"If you *wanted* to marry him, you should have married him a month ago and saved me the... the deuced pain of being scared you were dead, of missing you, of... of... no. Mr. Darcy has hurt you enough. And you are a sensible girl. Six months is enough time. You'll be past this... this destructive passion you have infatuated yourself with."

Mr. Bennet pointed at the carriage. "Now, Lizzy."

Darcy took her in his arms and passionately kissed her, before Mr. Bennet exclaimed, "Unhand my daughter, you ruffian!"

"I swear. I would wait until the end of times for you. And... it is not so very long. I will be there, the day of your birthday, I will be there for you."

Elizabeth tearfully nodded as Mr. Bennet pulled her up the drive and then pushed her onto the green cushions of their carriage.

*****

"Papa, please." The first words Elizabeth said to Mr. Bennet, even before he ordered the coachman to take off with their hired horses back down the long drive.

"No." Mr. Bennet sat comfortably in the carriage with an almost pleased light in his eye. "But, Lizzy, I am delighted — you are here again. You scared me, dear. What were you thinking, running off like that?"

"I... I needed to be away."

"I would have kept Mr. Darcy from bothering you further — which he would not want to do, and—"

"Papa, please let me go back. Give us permission. Be there when I marry."

"No."

The carriage rolled down the well-maintained road on Pemberley's lands, and then along the rutted and cramped road once they left the edge of Darcy's territory. Grey sticklike trees, not yet sprouting with spring. Cold brown fields. Hills and woods.

It would be so long. So long. She had waited for Darcy so long.

Mr. Bennet smiled at her, almost nervously when they had gone a half hour without a single word. "You aren't really unhappy — you had decided you did not want to marry him. I never should have allowed this to go forward at first. I have been full with guilt since. It will be a quite funny thing, when you come home."

"Has the scandal been terribly great?" Elizabeth flushed. "I would much rather visit as Mr. Darcy's wife. And Mama would be happy — I'll tell her that you are not allowing me to marry Mr. Darcy, and—"

"I can control your mother in a case where it really matters. I will not permit you to make a marriage that will be destructive of your future happiness just to keep from being bothered by her nerves. Lizzy, I care for you too deeply to do that. I was indolent, and I took the easiest course, the one that would keep me from facing society's disapproval, and that would keep your mother happy. But no more, when I saw your letters... when I realized what choices you had faced, and faced alone, without trusting me to guide you, because I would pick the choice easiest for myself, not best for you—"

"Papa."

"Not again. I'll not do it again."

"Oh, Papa."

"Perhaps I shall not always succeed, but I am determined to no longer be so indolent, to no longer allow myself to be moved to and fro by the urges of the moment and the question of what is easiest."

"As a general matter, Papa, I approve," Elizabeth began hopefully. If he really wanted to make her happy and do what was best for her, perhaps she *could* convince him that he should let her go back to Darcy. "I am happy, and Lydia, Kitty and Mary — and my mother — will benefit greatly from this choice. But I will marry Mr. Darcy."

"He hurt you. Hurt you so bad your only choice was to flee."

"I do not think that was *really* my only choice. I could have managed matters better... I wanted to be alone. I was hurt and..."

Mr. Bennet patted Elizabeth's hand. "But now everything will be happy and well again. And I have bought several new books you will want to read, and—"

"Why are you so convinced it would be a mistake for me to marry Mr. Darcy?"

Mr. Bennet rolled his eyes. "The two of you have too much animal passions betwixt you for things to be rational."

"We were apart for a full month, and he has replied and responded to every concern I had about his desire for our—"

"Only because he was desperate to know you!"

Elizabeth eyed her father who sat, wild haired and stiff.

"He *knew* me already, unless you mean..."

"Ha! A more desperate cur sniffing after a woman has never existed — once you are married, and the first months of passions pass, then he would regret the marriage. And you too, he is too serious, and too—"

"Mr. Darcy can control his impulses for the sake of honor. We have not... ah, well..."

"Lizzy, I know what it is like to be a man."

"You do not know what it is like to be Mr. Darcy. He doesn't... do such wild things. Not usually, and—"

BANG.

Elizabeth shrieked and shivered.

A horseman had got in front of the carriage. He shot a pistol into the air, and now he shouted at the coachman, "Stand ho! Stand ho! Stand and let me enter."

The coachman did stand down, and stop their carriage, intimidated by the guns the man carried.

Of course it was Darcy.

Elizabeth jumped from the carriage, before Mr. Bennet could grab to stop her from doing so, and Darcy leapt from his horse, and picked her up in his arms, and kissed her tightly as he swung her round and round.

"I cannot wait. I tried. For twenty minutes I tried, but I cannot wait. We must marry immediately. Waiting until your birthday. I do not want to. I want you, now."

"Oh, Fitzwilliam!" Elizabeth happily embraced him and smiled at him.

"Unhand my daughter! You true ruffian. Coming at us like a highwayman!"

"I am a highwayman, for I have stopped you to steal your greatest treasure. Elizabeth, will you marry me, though your father disapproves? We will be the happiest and most passionate couple in the world."

"Of course I will marry you."

"Well you can't! Not without my consent. You know that."

"Fitzwilliam, will you elope with me?" Elizabeth grinned at him, knowing that was his plan the instant she saw him on the back of his big brown stallion.

"It would be a scandal," Darcy replied with a dry tone. "Shouldn't we do anything to avoid a scandal?"

Elizabeth smiled brilliantly at him.

"My horse can carry both of us. We'll ride the whole way to Scotland."

"You are even less respectable than I thought — and I thought you were entirely unrespectable."

Darcy shrugged. "I am far too happy to be bothered by *that* anymore. I cannot even remember why I ever cared about scandals."

"My Lady." Darcy smiled at Elizabeth and lifted her up onto his saddle with his delightfully strong arms. It took him a moment of whispering to Marcus before the stallion became used to Elizabeth's presence. He used his powerful shoulders to lift his weight up and onto the saddle behind her. He settled himself with her quite in his lap, pressing her pert behind against his hips. He put his arms around Elizabeth and smelled the scent of her hair.

She smiled back at him and they kissed.

Then keeping her body squeezed against his, Darcy squeezed his knees and set his horse off towards Gretna Green.

Chapter Eighteen

"A quite excellent soup," "Mrs. Darcy" said, brushing her hand over the wrist of Mr. Darcy as she reached for the ladle to give herself an additional serving — Darcy had told the staff at the inn that Elizabeth was Mrs. Darcy when they entered. They were resting and eating while the staff of the inn prepared the post chaise they had rented.

Elizabeth and Darcy *wanted* to travel the whole two hundred miles from Pemberley to Gretna Green on horseback in one night, but to Darcy's disappointment, sitting in front of him on the saddle was not comfortable for Elizabeth in the slightest, and when she started complaining about the pain, they stopped at the next inn. She was already after just an hour of riding barely able to walk.

But her smile was amazing when he lifted her off the horse and set her on her unsteady feet.

Who would have expected that a perfect woman might *not* be an exemplary horsewoman? He should have guessed from how she *walked* three miles to Netherfield.

Alas, Fitzwilliam Darcy was much too in love to regret this strange form of Elizabeth's perfection.

Both of them openly looked each other's bodies up and down. Elizabeth desperately desired to kiss him again, to make love to him. She had wanted to be with him as a wife ever since that kiss in the room in the Netherfield Ball.

It had been fate.

They had sent the servants away to serve each other, and they were as good as married. Mr. Darcy was quite sure they would reach Gretna Green before twilight the next night.

There was no reason, except their scruples, not to enjoy the married embrace tonight, to not dock together, to not make their first attempt at basket making. From the look in his eyes, Darcy's scruples would not hold against the temptation she could offer — she knew *hers* would not hold if he made the slightest effort to overcome them. And if he didn't make such an effort, she would make the effort to overcome *his* scruples.

They had stopped talking as they happily stared into each other's eyes.

Darcy reached forward and brushed his fingers across her cheek, looking into Elizabeth's eyes.

Yes, she thought absently and leaned forward to kiss him, slowly sweetly and passionately, *tonight would be a very good night*.

His smell filled her mind. He had such a sweet spicy breath.

He wrapped his hand around the back of her head, and Elizabeth moaned and sighed as Darcy flicked his tongue along her lips. He tasted like the soup, and the tun of ale he'd been drinking from and so, so good.

Such soft wonderful lips.

Crash!

"Fitzwilliam! How *could you*!"

Georgiana stood in the doorway wearing the same fine blue travelling dress she'd worn when Georgiana found her in that town in the middle of England. Though the dress now had a line of lace and new sleeves that she had modified with Elizabeth. Georgiana's blond hair fluttered in the breeze created by how hard she'd thrown the door open. Behind Georgiana, Mrs. Annesley's plump friendly face smiled at them, and she waved.

Elizabeth and Darcy jumped back from each other and straightened their clothing which had somehow become unstraightened. Georgiana filled the doorway with her hands on her hips.

Several of the inn's curious staff gathered behind the two women to see what was happening. Quite poorly trained, thought Elizabeth, though she understood their curiosity.

"Well!" Georgiana stamped her foot. She was such a sweetheart. "What are you doing!"

"We are eloping," Mr. Darcy said to dear Georgiana with fondness in his tone and a surprising amount of dignity for a man whose cravat was entirely undone and hanging loosely around his neck — Elizabeth could not even remember undoing it. "Hence why we are on the road together and at this inn. I quite fear that we have decided to ignore all the disapproval of our families. Nothing you might say, Georgie, will dissuade us."

"I know *that*. Mr. Bennet told me all about it when he returned to Pemberley. And you *know* I support you. I am *so, so* happy that you and Lizzy *at last* are marrying — perfect for each other. Perfect — but *why* are you doing this?"

"Oh, Papa! He came back, what is he doing, how does he appear?"

"Mr. Bennet? He is fine. Established in the library hungrily looking over the books. I promised him he could stay as long as he wanted and read whatever he wished. Mrs. Reynolds will make sure he is fed if he goes too studious to remember for himself — but *why* are you doing this to *me*?"

Darcy looked at Elizabeth, who shrugged. Her heart still beat hard from the kiss and the door slam. "I confess, I am uncertain what you could be referring to if you are not put excessively out of temper by our plans to elope."

"You can't elope without your family." Georgiana's voice was both offended and whiney.

Elizabeth smiled and bit her lips mischievously. "Georgie, I believe that the definition of eloping *is* to marry without your family."

Georgiana blinked at this rebuttal and then snarled. "Well you still aren't doing it without *me*."

"I would never dream to," Darcy replied, jumping from his seat to take Georgiana's hand. "I shall be very glad to have *you* to witness us as we trespass Mr. Bennet's explicit and stated wish and make a mockery of parental authority."

Georgiana replied by raising one eyebrow when she looked at her brother.

"You can do it too!" Elizabeth exclaimed, filled with envy.

"What?"

Elizabeth poked Georgiana in the forehead above her full eyebrows. "Lift just one at a time! I've wanted to do it ever since I saw Darcy first do it — but he, the *brute*—" she happily kissed the shoulder of Darcy's coat "—insists the trick cannot be taught."

"Oh. Papa used to make that expression."

"I know."

"You can do it easily. I can teach you — if you want to know."

"I do! I do!" Elizabeth smiled happily, and wrapped her arm around her new sister's waist, feeling even more loved and at home than before — though some parts of her body were quite put out with Georgiana's appearance. They were only going to engage in convivial sport with each other *tomorrow* night, she was quite sure. But at least they could go the rest of the distance in the Darcy's comfortable, large and well-sprung carriage. "You are going to tell me all about how to raise just one eyebrow at a time during our trip to Scotland."

Darcy sighed. "And then you'll respond to everything I say, no matter how reasonable, with that same one eyebrow raised expression."

"You planned," Georgiana said, "to elope without me. You deserve such a punishment."

"You already are learning to tease him!" Elizabeth hugged her sister tightly. "I would never want to get married without you there."

She also hugged Mr. Darcy. "And now, to Scotland to find a blacksmith who will marry us over the anvil!"

Afterward:

This book was surprisingly easy to write. It was the first Pride and Prejudice I have written since I switched to a schedule of trying to focus on just writing four days a week, and I had two days of work while writing it where I produced more than ten thousand words of rough draft on each. Words which actually *seemed* good when I looked at them again after setting the text to the side for six weeks. *You* of course are the more important judge of whether what they turned into after further light editing was in fact good.

I am aware that some of you, though hopefully not many by proportion, will think this book is terrible.

I like this book, at least at the moment I am writing this afterward. Of course I *always* like my books right after I finish them. A terrible secret: I hope my love for my books is nothing like how I will love my children when I have them, since I do not love them all the same. I love the books who earn me more money more.

Except for *The Missing Prince*. You all can refrain from buying *that* book as much as you want, and I will still love the story. So we are really just talking about *The Trials* and *Mr. Darcy's Vow*. And some readers adore both of those books.

By the way, if you did like this book, please leave a review, especially if you are an early buyer who purchased *A Compromised Compromise* before there were a lot of reviews already written on the book. As an ardent reader you know how important reviews are to helping figure out what book to read next.

Also leave a review if you hated the book, I would beg, though, that if you must leave a negative review, to explain why you disliked it at greater length than "stupid, a crime against Jane Austen and the characters", since detailed negative reviews will help readers figure out if this is a book they will dislike, just like detailed positive reviews.

The delay between this book and *The Missing Prince* before this was caused by my decision that I wanted to write two or three novels that were not Pride and Prejudice before I wrote another Pride and Prejudice book. As it happened I only wrote one novel that wasn't a P&P variation, and spent the time during which I should have written another book and a half alternatively playing video games and throwing rough drafts and story concepts away.

Though, and this is one of those tidbits about writing process that I always enjoy reading about, it is extremely common for wasted work to turn out to not be wasted. For example, *Too Gentlemanly* was tossed to the side three times before I finally completed it, and *Mr. Darcy's Vow* was carved from the carcass of a planned forced marriage scenario.

Actually, the outline for this novel was found in my list of Pride and Prejudice ideas with a list of reasons for why it would be a bad idea to write. All disproven, I hope...

You can expect a lot more Pride and Prejudice books from me, for at least the next year or so. I am right now alternating every five weeks between Pride and Prejudice projects and other projects, and so far I have enjoyed this schedule a great deal, and I have two rough drafts in process, so I'm not sure which will be published next (or even if *either* will be), but I in neither case am I randomly spinning my wheels without making forward progress.

So I am reasonably confident it won't be another nine months before my next P&P variation comes out.

A specific note on one influence for this novel: There was a ridiculous little story on Dwiggie that I read years and years ago titled, "Whilst in their cradles" which had an insane Lady Catherine stand in her daughter's cradle and order Lady Anne Darcy to stand in her son's cradle, and then declare that the two should marry. The line of inspiration from that story to Darcy imagining such a situation is fairly clear.

Finally, I want to urge you to donate with me to help those suffering in extreme poverty. Year by year due to economic growth and the efforts of people like you and me, the world is becoming a better place. Fewer people die each year because of starvation, or lack of access to antibiotics and basic medical care. Maternal death rates are steadily falling around the world, and I think there are no countries left where it is more dangerous to have or be a child today than it was for Jane Austen.

The world is becoming a better place, and it is possible that within our lifetimes we will see extreme poverty end. Be part of this great change. Be part of bringing medical care to those in war zones and in extreme poverty. I support Doctors Without Borders because they are an efficient and transparent organization, but there are other groups who can make your money do an enormous amount of good. So pick one, and join me in creating the future we want to see.

Make a choice to donate some amount of money you can spare, whether ten dollars a month, or one percent of your income, or whatever you can manage, so that you can be part of the world becoming a better, happier place.

Timothy Underwood

Budapest, November 2018

ABOUT THE AUTHOR

I am from California, but I currently live in Budapest with my fiancée. I first discovered Pride and Prejudice on a long day of travel out of Mexico as a teenager. I recall being very impressed with myself for getting the jokes. I read a lot of nineteenth century literature that year, of which Austen and Charlotte Bronte, of course, were my favorites. It was years later that I discovered and repeatedly binge read Pride and Prejudice fanfiction.

Now I get to add to the pile of fanfiction able to binge – and I love it when I get messages from people telling me that they are binging on my books.

If you liked this book, leave a review. It is a way of helping other people find books they liked.

I can be reached at timothyunderwood.author@gmail.com.

Made in the USA
Middletown, DE
05 March 2020